ELIZABETH BROMWELL

Chronicles of an Expat Spy

By

KATHRYN RAAKER

&

Lawrence L. Allen

Kathryn Raaker

http://www.kathrynraaker.com

http://www.letsjusttalkradio.com

Cover Design: Charlotte Rinderknecht

Lawrence L. Allen

http://www.hangneckridge.com/elizabeth_bromwell

ISBN: 978-0-9915826-2-4

Chantry Farm

Chantry Farm was the beloved home of the Raaker family from 1978 to 1981 while on assignment in the United Kingdom. A hunting lodge built in 1591, it later became the country home of Lord Allister Graham. It serves as the inspiration for the fictional grandmother's quarters on the Avebury English country estate in the Elizabeth Bromwell series.

St. John the Baptist,
Campsea Ashe

ACKNOWLEDGEMENTS

First and foremost I thank my Lord and Savior for giving me eternal life and inspiring me to write this book. I'm grateful to my parents for bringing me into the world and giving me guidance and encouragement to pursue an artistic career. Thanks to my editor, partner and dear husband Bill, who supported this project from conception and gave me the courage to continue. My children Robert, Jeff and Jenny, and all our grandchildren, my daughters-in-law and son-in-law for listening and giving their undying support to the project. My sister, Mary, for all her love, creative contributions and encouragement to write more. Edwin Linz, my dearest cousin, and Best-Selling author himself, for creative advice. Thanks to my co-author Lawrence Allen—without him this book would not exist. And special thanks to Robin Graham, Pam Bell, Linda Cadman, David & Yvonne Hall and Eileen & Peter Hall for their friendship and for their help with research for telling this story.

DEDICATION

This book is dedicated to my Lord and Savior; in loving memory of my parents; to my husband Bill and our three children Robert, Jeff and Jenny; all our grandchildren; our daughters-in-law and son-in-law; and all our friends around the world.

CHAPTER 1

"Houston, Tranquility Base here. The Eagle has landed."

Elizabeth Bromwell watched the ghostly black and white images of the first moon landing flickering from a television set above the foot of her hospital bed. Houston: "Be advised, there are lots of smiling faces in this room. And all over the world."

But while the entire world might have been smiling at that moment, she wasn't. For Elizabeth was on the edge of despair: her life seemingly at its end, before it had hardly begun. Recovering from typhoid fever, which she'd contracted three weeks earlier in the very same hospital while having an emergency hysterectomy, allowed ample time for her to take stock. She was a recently divorced Catholic girl, age 23 with a toddler, no visible means of support, who six months earlier had finally escaped from her miserable marriage in a hard-fought divorce. Her ex-husband had thus far failed to play any meaningful part in their son's life or cooperate with her request for an annulment. While she longed for her impending discharge from the hospital, she was also terrified by it. What on earth would she do once she walked out the hospital door? What kind of life could she possibly rebuild on such unstable ground? She had no idea.

Elizabeth's parents told her that their door was always open to her and her son Jacob, but Elizabeth refused to return home. Her pride always got in the way. That, and returning to her parents' constant bickering made returning home a last resort. Her father was a struggling musician and they met in a war time-factory. Her mother came from a well to do family and had married him against their wishes. Estranged from her family, they lived a rollercoaster life: married, divorced, and remarried. They couldn't avoid arguing about everything, but most often about money.

An adult was needed in the family and Elizabeth was it. Of her six siblings, she was the oldest. And while her mother worked and father was away on band gigs she began cooking at age ten, and by age eleven was managing the family's affairs. Cooking, cleaning, ironing, getting the other children ready for school, going to school herself and trying to study—it was all too much for a child. So she grew up. "We're like slaves, serving the family," she once complained to her sister.

Elizabeth wanted to run away from it all as soon as she could. And so, when at age 19 her first husband proposed marriage, she saw it as her way out—and took it. And that was the biggest mistake of her young life. At the end of her rope in divorce court three years later she threw herself on the mercy of the court, telling the judge: "He had a lame horse and a dog, and he loved and treated those animals better than he treated me. Even that old Tennessee Walker with a bad hoof."

Elizabeth paused to listen to Neil Armstrong's mother answer a reporter who asked: "Mrs. Armstrong, what were your feelings at the moment that Apollo 11 was coming toward the moon."

Elizabeth felt a tear well up in her eye when mother Armstrong replied: "Well, I was just hoping and praying that everything would go well. I must say praise God, from Whom all blessings flow."

Elizabeth had also hoped and prayed that everything would go well—with her marriage. Indeed, the Catholic church had gone to great lengths to ensure the Lord had blessed her marriage. But for Elizabeth only pain, disappointment and fear flowed from her short, failed marriage. And while it was being reported on television that the President of the United States expressed that they were in the greatest moment of our time, that day in divorce court six months earlier would continue to be the worst moment of her time: being *granted* a divorce. Yes, she violated a tenet of her faith, but she also failed at the most important goal she had for her life—providing for a stable and happy family.

And Elizabeth hung her head to fully cry when a reporter asked Neil Armstrong's wife if she had said a special prayer at the time of the landing. "No, I didn't say any extra special prayers at that time," said Mrs. Armstrong. "My faith is with me always." But was Elizabeth's faith still with *her*?

Elizabeth hurriedly dried her eyes and composed herself before responding to the knock at the door. She felt her heart lift as her priest, Father Bartholomew, entered her hospital room. They talked and she opened her heart.

"Father, I've completely lost confidence in myself," she pleaded. Since the divorce she'd had a traffic accident that put her on disability. Her chronic over eating to ease the pain and boredom only left her heavier than she'd ever been—and even more depressed and less self-confident. "And on top of all this I feel ashamed in the eyes of God for my divorce."

But Father Bartholomew was a good priest, an understanding person and a good listener. His gentle manner always put Elizabeth at ease and gave her hope. When he spoke, she felt the love and forgiveness of Christ fill the room—projected through the geniality of Father Bartholomew. She felt it, and she felt better about herself and her prospects.

* * *

A few months after her discharge from Corpus Christi's CHRISTUS Spohn Hospital Elizabeth was puttering around home, flipping through bills, straightening up here and there. She kept her son Jacob busy and out of the way by plopping him in front of the TV in her bedroom. Sesame Street was a new show just for kids that he seemed to enjoy.

Elizabeth was starting a new job the following Monday. She laid her final disability check on the counter under her keys—so she wouldn't forget to cash it at the bank that morning after her neighbor, Mrs. Evans, came by to pick up Jacob for the day. In the afternoon, it was off to the church for her weekly ritual—speaking and praying together with Father Bartholomew.

She returned home from the bank just before noon to find a note stuffed into her mobile home's screen door that held a simple message: *Call this number right away.* She recognized it, it was the number for her Church. What could be so urgent that the priest would send someone over with a note? If he was cancelling their afternoon meeting, why didn't they just write that on the note? A tearful Mrs. Grassley, the church treasurer, answered the phone: "It's Father Bartholomew, Elizabeth…" she wept, "…he drowned this morning. He was swimming in the ocean and…" Elizabeth dropped the phone and collapsed to the floor. Her eyes came to rest on a bottle of Vodka she kept for guests. A half hour later it was half empty and Elizabeth was passed out on the couch.

Late afternoon creeping sunbeams that had finally made their way across the room to her eyelids, together with Mrs. Evans' banging on her screen door, brought Elizabeth to consciousness. She managed to rise to her feet to open the door for Mrs. Evans and Jacob, just before running to the sink and spending the next quarter hour purging the contents of her stomach.

"Well, that's not going to work for me," she said aloud as she gingerly sipped at a glass of water that Mrs. Evans had handed to her. Elizabeth, having concluded that she couldn't drink, vowed to never drink like that again. "Where is Jacob?"

"He's fine, dear. I put him down for his afternoon nap." She stroked Elizabeth's hair back over her shoulder. "What on earth were you thinking?"

"I was thinking that I just wanted to end it all. I wanted out. Out of this mess," Elizabeth's strained diaphragm and abdominal muscles ached a bit with each word. "Out of life altogether."

"Why on earth would you want that, sweetie?"

She explained what had happened. "He was my only hope," she uttered before the tears came. Mrs. Evans took her head to her shoulder and held it there. "He was the person who was…he was keeping me level. He was what was enabling me to put one foot in front of another."

Mrs. Evans began rocking Elizabeth back and forth. She didn't have an answer for her.

"Why has God taken him from me?"

"I don't know, dear." Mrs. Evans joined her with a tear. "Perhaps you should ask God."

* * *

What a difference a week makes, Elizabeth thought as she pulled up to the church. She had a new job, was dressed in new clothes that were a size smaller. She felt alert and confident having already earned praise from her new boss after less than a full week on the job. She was ready to meet the new priest who would fill in for Father Bartholomew until his permanent replacement arrived.

The interim priest was an older man with an Irish accent. Like she did with Father Bartholomew, Elizabeth poured her heart out to him. She shared her hopes and dreams for a normal life—about one day winning an annulment and remarrying. But the old priest's expression betrayed his words to follow: "You're divorced now. The church will not bless a second marriage without an annulment—until then you can't remarry in the Church. Technically, you aren't even supposed to date."

Elizabeth felt knocked down again. If this is the way it was going to be, she wondered if she should search for answers elsewhere.

CHAPTER 2

The day had arrived. Elizabeth finally got back into her pre-pregnancy clothing…comfortably. She'd let her sandy blond hair grow out, her energy level was back at peak and she was raring to go. She now commanded a respectable sales territory and with commissions that brought home nearly three times what she was making when she first started. She was moving out of the mobile home park and into an apartment complex that had a daycare center for Jacob, and rent low enough that she could save for a down payment to buy her own place one day. But even this would not be without difficulty.

Although she complied with all the terms of her mobile home rental agreement, the mobile home park manager refused to return her deposit. Every week like clockwork she'd see a couple of Cadillacs pull up to the parks' office and the scruffy manager in his dirty t-shirt talking with the well-dressed visitors. They always looked to Elizabeth like they were up to no good. So, days before she was to move into the apartment she marched over to the Cadillacs.

"This…" she looked the manager up and down, "…*man*, refuses to give me my security deposit back. I demand to meet with your boss." Everyone was now looking at her in amazement. All of five-foot four and a half, she stood her ground with her fists on her hips. The manager rolled his eyes over his fat cheeks. Two of the well-dressed men looked at each other and shrugged.

"Okay," one of them said. "Get in," he gestured while another of them opened a car door for her. Within minutes they were sitting at a local diner with another man who was already seated.

"Look," Elizabeth caught herself. "Sir, please, I don't know who you are, but that manager of yours is trying to stiff me out of my security deposit. Now, I know that a hundred bucks may not be a lot of money to you, but it is a heck of a lot of money to me."

The man, clearly the boss, relit his cigar and gestured as if to say: *keep going.*

"I'm a girl with an ex-husband who isn't cooperating or doing his share. I've been working hard to move into an apartment complex nearby that has daycare for my son...you know, so I don't have to impose on my neighbors all the time. I don't want any handouts, only what I'm due."

The man with the cigar leaned over, offered his hand to Elizabeth and cordially introduced himself. After discovering that her father was a regular performer in some of his clubs, they went on talking. A half hour later they were laughing together and practically family.

"I apologize for any inconvenience caused. Here..." He reached for his wallet.

"No." Elizabeth stopped him by putting her hand on his arm. "I want that manager to give it back to me. Just so he knows that he can't take advantage of any other women like me."

"Yeah, sure. We can do it that way," sitting back. "Do you want us to talk to your ex-husband for you?"

Elizabeth was tempted. "No, I can handle him. But thank you anyway." Her ex would never know how close he came.

She took his business card when offered: "Highland Park Properties. I'll remember that." She put it into her purse for safe keeping.

"Give my regards to your father, will you?"

In addition to impressing organized crime captains, Elizabeth discovered that she was really good at sales, and having finally found something that she was good at, she pursued it with all her vigor. Between work, volunteering at the church, raising Jacob, and looking in on her parents occasionally, she had little time for anything else. So, when a neighbor and friend suggested a double date, hers being a blind date, Elizabeth was hesitant.

"He's a military officer from some base in Colorado Springs..." her friend taunted. "He's some kind of special forces...Green Beret or something."

Elizabeth sighed. "Oh, I don't know..." timidly. "I've just got so much going on right now. I really don't..."

"Liz, you're almost 25 years old. How long are you going to wait? And the older Jacob gets, the harder it will be for a man to accept him...and you. Know what I mean?"

"A military officer, huh?"

"Yep. And those guys are college educated. And after their 20-years-'n-out they get great benefits for life from the government—and then start a whole new career."

"Let me think about it."

* * *

The Captain held the rear car door for Elizabeth's friend while Major Cliff Holt held the front passenger door for Elizabeth after the men pulled up to the apartment complex in Major Holt's rental car. The phrase *officer and a gentleman* went through Elizabeth's mind as Major Holt gently closed the door beside her. She could tell it was going to be a very nice evening.

Two weeks later, on the advice from a friend, Elizabeth found herself receiving consultation from another priest—an expert on the annulment process.

"What is troubling you, my dear?"

"Honestly, father. I don't know what to do. I'm divorced. And I met a man a couple of months ago who I really like a lot. He treats me so well and accepts me for who I am."

"I see." The priest paused. "Those are good things, right?"

"No! I'm petrified." Elizabeth lowered her voice. "Last weekend he invited me to his home in Colorado Springs. A military base. He couldn't wait for me to take a commercial flight, so he sent me to a local airport and I went up by private plane. It was my first time flying anywhere."

"Did your child join you?"

"He paid for a babysitter…can you believe that?" The priest nodded. "We had a wonderful time. I was there for 3 days. And he was a perfect gentleman the entire time."

"It sounds like a good start to a healthy relationship to me. What are your concerns, my child?"

"Well, he wanted me to come live with him, there in Colorado Springs."

"Living together before marriage is a sin."

"No, I know that. That's just the thing: I think he was going to ask me to marry him."

"I see. Again, that's a good thing, right?"

Elizabeth hung her head for a moment and caught her fingers fidgeting with her nails. "I don't know, father. I mean, I think he was going to propose to me. And in a very amazing way. He leads paratroopers and the very last day before I went home, he took me up in a jump plane. He told me he had something very important to ask me, but that he'd only ask me while we were freefalling." Elizabeth caught her breath. "I mean, what else could it be, right? So, we were at the door together and we were ready to jump and…"

"Were you afraid to jump?"

"No. I mean, yes, I was afraid to jump, but I could have done it. That's not the problem. What I was afraid of was…"

"You were afraid of what he was going to say to you?"

"Terrified."

The priest gave her time to reflect and compose her thoughts.

"I'm terrified of making another mistake, father. As exciting and wonderful as Cliff, is… " Elizabeth stiffened and straightened up in her seat. "Since I was the age of ten I've served everyone around me. My mother and father. My siblings. Then my husband." Her voice strengthened. "And now I'm just finding myself for the very first time in my life. I don't want to give that up."

"I understand."

"Independence is…freedom," she went on. "No matter how loving and how much a gentleman Cliff could be, I don't want to be dependent on anyone."

"So, you didn't jump?" She could sense the priest's piqued curiosity.

"No. I flew home that afternoon."

"Do you now regret your decision?"

"We tried a long-distance relationship for a few more months, but I could see right away that it wasn't going to work. I love my independence, my friends, my customers, my job…and I'm really good at it too. I finally have something of my own and I just don't want to let it go." Elizabeth continued, sharing her family history and her concern that she may never achieve her life's goal of providing for a stable and happy family.

"Elizabeth, you came here for a reason. It sounds like you want to renew your faith: both in the church *and* maybe a future marriage."

"Yes, father. I need your guidance."

* * *

It was Elizabeth's only practical escape: her uncle's ranch out near Three Rivers, Texas. With Jacob asleep in his car seat next to her, as the two of them plowed through the rain north, along US-281, she had only a sore chin, bone-chipped elbow and her thoughts about the past week to keep her company. And those thoughts were nightmares. It was Sunday morning and the road was deserted. The only cars she saw along the way were those crowded into church parking lots. Elizabeth would miss Sunday church for the first time in as long as she could remember.

The week began on Monday with her parents' car accident that nearly killed them. A drunk driver jumped a median and collided with them head on. Both her father's thumbs were broken owing to the impact and his 10-and-2 o'clock grip on the steering wheel, and he had a cracked knee-cap from impacting the lower dashboard. Time would tell if the injuries to his hands would affect his musical career. Fortunately, Elizabeth's mother had insisted that they order the car with both lap and shoulder belts: a decision that left her mother with only a cracked collarbone and bruised knees. Without those safety belts, it would have been much, much worse. When Elizabeth left them Monday evening, sharing a hospital room, they were already bickering. They were going to be okay.

On Tuesday, when Elizabeth arrived to substitute for a teacher at the local middle school, she had planned to visit her parents at the hospital after the end of the school day. She didn't know that she would be seeing them much earlier that day.

Elizabeth started teaching part time: something she'd always dreamt of. She substituted twice a week at a school with a horrible reputation of being in the wrong neighborhood. "Don't turn your back on these little hoodlums for a minute," one of the teachers warned her first day on the job. That morning she found out why. One of the girls she'd disciplined in class early that morning came up behind her on the school stairs landing and pushed her. She fell face first down the stairs. It was 11:45 AM when she walked into her parents' hospital room with a fat lip, a bruised chin and her arm in a sling. She was waiting for x-ray results to determine the condition of her elbow.

When Wednesday rolled around Elizabeth was exhausted. Her sore elbow kept her up all night—she just couldn't find a comfortable sleeping position for it. It was nearly four o'clock in the afternoon when the phone rang and woke her up.

"Miss Bromwell? This is Private Jennings. We met when you were here in Colorado Springs. I'm Major Cliff Holt's assistant."

"Hold on a moment, please." Elizabeth sat up and composed herself. Though she'd put a damper on Cliff's intentions, they had stayed in touch with weekly calls— sometimes twice a week or more. He was charming and persistent and they could always find things to talk about for hours. But Elizabeth had made up her mind and that was that. "Yes, Private Jennings, how are you? Please, put me through."

"Uh, Miss Bromwell, mam…" the private said cautiously. "There's been a training accident. Major Holt's parachute didn't properly deploy," there was a pause on both ends of the line. "He was killed, mam." She cried herself to sleep.

Elizabeth pulled herself together by the time she arrived first thing Thursday morning at the disciplinary meeting. The Principal and Vice Principle were there to determine what was to be done with the student who'd pushed her down the stairs two days earlier. "The family has filed a complaint," the principle began. Clearing his throat: "…against you."

"Did you threaten the girl with detention, in front of the entire class, if she didn't comply?" the Vice Principle followed up.

"Absolutely, I did," Elizabeth responded. "She was using profanity in my class and made an obscene gesture to me when I called on her to answer a history question."

"Well, her parents said you singled their daughter out all morning, humiliating her, and then threatened her in front of her classmates."

Elizabeth gathered her things. "I see where this is going," she stood up. "Don't bother firing me. I quit."

Friday's relief came in the form of a busy work day that took her mind off the craziness and tragedy of the week. Elizabeth was able to operate without her sling, but her elbow would be tender for another couple of weeks. The fat lip had gone down, and bruised chin covered nicely with make-up. The customers she saw that day were none the wiser. At least she wouldn't have to explain the awkward circumstances of her "accident," or worse, lie to them. The teachers at Jacob's pre-school informed Elizabeth that he had another great day and that he was adapting well to school. Elizabeth showered him with praise. She was grateful that Jacob was doing well and the two of them played "driver" all the way home: Elizabeth with her hands on the steering wheel and Jacob with the toy wheel attached to his car seat. "Just like mommy, huh?" Elizabeth said just before rounding the corner to the entrance of her apartment complex. Both her and Jacob's mouths dropped open. Their apartment building was on fire. Residents were standing outside watching and waiting for the firetrucks that moments later arrived in a flurry of lights and sirens. She saw her neighbor, rolled down her window and yelled to her. "Did everyone get out?"

"Yes, we think so, thank God," the neighbor said, jogging over. "I was in the lobby when the superintendent pulled the fire alarm. We went floor to floor, door to door. We think everyone got out. Elizabeth and Jacob lived on the top floor—which was entirely engulfed in flames.

Elizabeth drove to her parent's house. Her parents

were home from the hosptial. Father was awkwardly attempting to play the guitar with his thumbs in splints. He winced at the pain, but kept on going. Mother was sitting in front of the TV watching reruns.

"My apartment burned down." Her parents looked at her in silent shock. "I'm going to go get my old room ready for Jacob and me." On her way upstairs she passed her father's bar and thought to reach for the bottle of Vodka there. But she could still smell the *vomit-highball* from the last time she tried to anesthetize herself that way.

By Sunday, she needed an escape: her uncle's ranch.

"Oh Lord," she said aloud as they emerged into sunshine from beneath the shadow of rain clouds that had left US-281 a steaming strip of blacktop, snaking across the featureless Texas plain for as far as the eye could see. "You have sent so many into the wilderness," she prayed, as she looked over at the angelic tranquil look on her sleeping son's face. "You have told us through scripture that between where we are now, and where we receive Your promises and blessings, there is always a wilderness that must be crossed." She took a deep breath and sighed. Tears clouded her vision. "I know that you put these trials before us to grow our faith and our understanding of You. And to bring us closer to You..." Elizabeth couldn't go on. The words just stopped coming.

Drying her eyes, she composed herself. She saw Jacob's head out of the corner of her eye roll down off his shoulder. She looked over and saw that he was awake and smiling at her. She smiled back. He was staring out through the windshield and she followed his gaze to a double rainbow, both of which ended near where their road met the horizon. It was the first double rainbow she'd ever seen. And upon seeing it, the emotions that boiled in her heart suddenly changed from despair to optimism. She didn't know why.

CHAPTER 3

"Honey, it's your aunt Estelle," her voice cackled over the receiver. "I'm coming down to see you and the family. But I want to make sure we spend a little time together, just the two of us."

Everyone loved eccentric old Aunt Estelle. She was Elizabeth's favorite relative—her idol of sorts. She lived in Manhattan in New York City, was a career woman whose resume included film arts, real estate, world travel, publishing, entertainment and just about every other exciting thing Elizabeth could imagine. When she picked Aunt Estelle up at the airport later that week she was of course wearing the latest New York fashion: a pastel polyester bell bottom pants suit. She used a lady's-style fedora hat to tame her trademark frizzy hair.

"Oh, my dear, it is so good to see you," she hugged Elizabeth tightly in the airport reception area.

During two different summers Elizabeth had taken the train to New York City and each time stayed ten days with her Aunt Estelle. She worked for a publisher in the Flatiron district at the time. Elizabeth could still remember the smell of ink and binding glues at the city print shop her aunt took her to one time. Aunt Estelle was a confident and independent woman, with a big personality and voice with which to express it. And when she sang, as she often did around her apartment, she sounded to Elizabeth so much like Ethyl Merman that she was convinced that she was doing an impersonation of her. Especially when she sang "Everything's Coming Up Roses." Every time she performed that number, Elizabeth would pull the curtains over her open windows so no one could see.

Estelle stayed in a hotel on the beach and visited friends and family in Corpus Christi by day, while Elizabeth was working. In the evenings, the two of them would chat on her balcony overlooking the ocean. It was a time that Aunt Estelle would always turn her undivided attention to Elizabeth.

"Staying single the rest of your life will never do, sweetheart," Estelle pleaded.

"You never married."

"I just haven't met the right man yet, dear. Not for a lack of trying," she said, taking a long tug on her wine.

Elizabeth quietly smiled. Her Aunt Estelle was her father's older sister and likely in excess of 60 years old. Did she really hold out hope for finding "Mr. Right," or was she just saying that for her benefit?

"Now I want you to know that I've made arrangements with a close friend I have here Corpus Christi for you to meet her nephew. He's a good Catholic boy. He's your age. I haven't met him myself, but I trust my friend's judgement implicitly."

Another blind date? Elizabeth didn't know if she was ready to meet someone.

"I understand that there is a Jolly Roger Festival or something right here on the beach this weekend. His name is Carson Jordon and he'd be delighted to take you there," she said with finality. "It's all been arranged."

*   *   *

The Jolly Roger Festival was a Corpus Christi tradition, one that Elizabeth had always thought was a little too goofy for her tastes. But she didn't want to let Aunt Estelle down. A dashing man with a military-style haircut, black rim glasses and a suit, a look that was completely out of sync with the early '70s styles—just the way Elizabeth liked it—walked up to her standing by the designated ticket booth.

"Are you Elizabeth?" He looked genuinely pleased to meet her.

After confirming he was Carson Jordon, and that their aunts were old friends going back to school days, they began walking along the boardwalk that cradled the Jolly Roger Festival.

"Do you feel like going to this thing?" Carson asked, watching adults dressed in pirate costumes walk buy drinking and laughing.

"I thought you wanted to meet here?"

"That was my Aunt's idea. Hey, I know a diner where we can get a great milkshake. Whaddya' say?"

Elizabeth didn't know why, but she was compelled to pour her heart out to Carson in that diner. Perhaps it was because he was a great listener—he seemed to hang on her every word. Perhaps it was their mutual love of children—Carson was a baseball coach and mentored disadvantaged boys from the city as a Big Brother. Or, that he was the oldest from a big working-class family too—and had to grow up early. How could she not open up to him? By the time they'd walked miles to her apartment building's entrance that evening it was nearly midnight.

"You know, this date screwed up my pool night," Carson said matter-of-factly. Looking down at his feet: "But I'm kind of glad it did."

"Me too. Thanks for listening," she said, giving Carson a kiss on the cheek before turning and going up the stairs.

Carson insisted that Elizabeth bring Jacob along on their next date, and the three of them were inseparable for the next three dates after that—which occurred all in the space of a week. Elizabeth loved to watch Carson and Jacob together. Carson was a natural with boys. Jacob was somewhat wary of most men, taking a long time to establish trust. Elizabeth suspected it was because he was estranged from his natural father. But there was none of that with Carson: they instantly took a liking to each other. And Jacob couldn't stop talking about him when they were separated.

For their sixth date, Carson asked Elizabeth to leave Jacob with his grandparents, as she'd done on the first date. He told her it was because they'd be going out for a special evening that he'd planned for them. As Elizabeth walked toward Carson who was standing at their usual meeting place beside the city-center fountain, a hoard of butterflies rose in her abdomen. Carson was impeccably dressed as always. But instead of holding his trademark pipe in his hand, he was cradling another object. A small box.

He said only one thing when she arrived: "Will you marry me?"

Elizabeth hung her head in sadness. "You need to know something, Carson. I've been unable to get an annulment from my first husband. He won't cooperate. We couldn't be married in the Church—at least with the sacraments."

"Will you marry me," Carson repeated without hesitation.

Elizabeth sighed deeply. "There were complications after Jacob…" she couldn't control her tears. "I had to have a hysterectomy, Carson. I can't have any more children."

Carson paused, momentarily dazed as if he'd been punched in the solar plexus. He shook it off, cleared his throat, pursed his lips and replanted his feet. "Will you marry me."

* * *

"It's called Leith Sports & Leisure Engineering, plc. It's a British company. They build golf courses and resorts, amusement parks, things of that nature. They badly need irrigation engineers. Their US office is in San Diego. Besides, all the action right now for golf courses is around San Diego," Carson said between bites of barbequed chicken.

"But, San Diego, Carson? Oh, I don't know," Elizabeth said sipping her coffee while leaning against their apartment's kitchenette.

"It right by the ocean, just like Corpus Christi. A better ocean, too. The Pacific. You can surf there."

"Surf," Elizabeth scoffed. "But we have plans here. We're going to buy a house…"

"Come on. It'll be fun," he said with a smile. "Hey, you wanna learn how to surf, Jacob? It'll be cool…like the beach boys!" Jacob thought San Diego was a cool idea too.

It was barely six months after the Justice of the Peace

married them that Elizabeth was faced with a choice: pick up her life and move, or hold back her husband's career advancement. But what of her own career? Her company didn't do business in California. She'd have to start all over again. She thought of that little fixer-upper within sight of the ocean that they'd been looking at, then watched as Jacob jumped up on the kitchen chair and pretended to surf—with Carson singing *Surfin' USA*.

"We'll take it," said Elizabeth when they finished walking through the mobile home model in Escondido, California. "We'll let you know where we'd like it delivered before the week is out."

"Imagine that," Elizabeth said as they started their drive back to the San Diego motel they'd been at for the past week. "For the first time, a brand new mobile home. We get to pick our carpet, our counters…and your room Jacob, did you see it? It so big!"

Though they would visit several mobile home parks in San Diego, there was only one that would do: the one right on the ocean. The mobile home park's management office was going to call them back to let them know whether there'd be any immediate availability. A flashing red light on the motel phone let them know that they had a message at the motel's front desk.

Elizabeth called the management office and was told there were no vacancies for the foreseeable future. "Uh, huh. I see," Elizabeth cleared her throat, looking at Carson. "Tell me, what's the name of the company that owns your facility?" she said tucking the phone between her ear and shoulder while grabbing a pencil and pad. "Oh, Highland Park Properties. I see. Thank you very much," she put the pencil down, smiled broadly at Carson who gave her a quizzical look. She began digging through her purse until she found the cigar-smoking gangster's business card.

"This was always my favorite property too," the cigar-smoking gangster said as they watched an old, unkept mobile home being towed away from a prime spot in the San Diego seaside mobile home park. "I don't know why the manager kept this piece of junk here…it's an eyesore, you know? Maybe it was his love shack, or something," he said with a smile and a wink. "I understand that yours is arriving this afternoon. May your home be blessed, sweetheart," pinching her cheek.

"Thank you so much. You don't know what this means to us."

"Hey, I was in the neighborhood…" he shrugged. "Anything for your father's little girl."

It wasn't two weeks before Elizabeth had their move completed, Jacob in school and time on her hands. And that just wouldn't do. She had to go back to teaching. There was a federally funded school in the center of San Diego that was advertising for substitute teachers. "It's kind of a rough neighborhood," the principle warned. "The girls are worse than the boys."

Elizabeth laughed. "Don't worry. I've been there before. I can handle it." Elizabeth wondered if she had just uttered famous last words.

On her first day of teaching Elizabeth had two girls escorted from class to the principal's office before 11 AM. That earned her a guest of honor invitation to a *gang stomp party* in the hallway, which fortunately for Elizabeth ended with only a knuckle sandwich: that earned the misfit who threw the punch, Kayla, a week's suspension. When asked if she wanted to file a formal complaint Elizabeth said that she only wanted the girl to serve detention with her three days a week for two months.

"You think you've come from hard knocks, girl?" she told Kayla her first day of detention. "Let me tell you, you don't know the half of it." And Elizabeth proceeded to read her the riot act. "Well, there is one thing I know you've got going for you: your big mouth. It takes one to know one." During each detention Elizabeth taught Kayla the basics of debate. And after she got to know the other girls in the class, she hand-picked three others and formed the middle school's girls debate team. Even after Kayla's detention was served, they all met three days a week after school to practice debate. Elizabeth didn't tell the girls that she'd signed them up for a debate competition with other San Diego neighborhood schools until the new semester began in January.

"We can't do this, Mrs. Jordon," one of the girls said nervously. "Our school...nobody ever does nothing from our school."

"Nobody ever does *anything* from our school. And there is always a first time for everything."

Kayla looked at Elizabeth, then looked at the other girls. "I can't believe you guys think we're not as good as those girls from those other schools." She knew Elizabeth was focused on her at that moment, but tried not to betray it. "We can do this. We're as good as anyone else. Believe me, it takes one to know one." Kayla looked at Elizabeth and smiled. Elizabeth's heart soared as she heard her words now being repeated by Kayla.

Their debate team came in third amongst a field of ten schools.

* * *

"Minneapolis!" shrieked Elizabeth. "We'll freeze up there."

"Hey, that's where the action is now. They play golf in cold climates too, you know."

"I know, but we've only been here for two years. My debate team is the #1 team in its bracket in San Diego now. We're going on to all-state competition in the fall."

Carson knew this was a blow for Elizabeth. "I'm heading the entire irrigation team up there. We can afford to buy an actual house." He teased. "Houses up there— real houses—are one third the price they are here in San Diego.

Elizabeth paused for a moment. This was Carson's opening.

"Come on, it'll be fun. With the change of seasons and all?" Carson reasoned. "It's where Mary Tyler Moore does her TV show from. You can even watch Ted Baxter do the news every night."

"Ted Baxter's a jerk," Jacob added with a degree of sincerity that made both Elizabeth and Carson smile to each other.

It was the second-to-last day before the end of the school year: the mobile home was sold, the moving truck has pulled away that morning, and it was Elizabeth's last day teaching before they piled into the family car and made the 2,000-mile journey to Minneapolis. She was informed in the teacher's lounge that she would be filling in for an English class that day. The bell rang and she made her way to the classroom. When she opened the door and saw a big hand-made banner that said: *Thank You!* The classroom erupted with a cheer from students in her debate class and many from other classes: "We'll miss you Mrs. Jordon."

Elizabeth was concerned that Jacob would be traumatized by losing all his friends in the move, but he seemed to take the move in stride. During the drive up to Minneapolis he was intensely curious about each place they passed through. She studied him watching the country pass by outside the car window: he was transfixed. That's one less thing to worry about.

Summer in Minneapolis was beyond their family's expectations. The lush rolling hills. Lakes at every turn. They found a church they liked: a very good parish with an outstanding young priest. They enrolled Jacob in Catholic school. And, of course, they bought their first house.

It was at the beginning of their second year in Minnesota that her ex-husband called. "I need an annulment," he said over the phone. Just like that. He had met someone who was also a devout Catholic and who insisted that he annul his previous marriage so they could be married in the Church.

"Listen buster, for nearly ten years I was seeking an annulment and you didn't have the time of day for me and Jacob. And now you need it and you just snap your fingers and expect me to jump for you, huh?" Elizabeth wanted nothing more badly than to have her first marriage annulled, but she knew she had him over a barrel. "I don't want anything but what we're due," she said in a business-like voice. "We need to talk."

Elizabeth Jordon had found a home in her Minnesota community. She was a full-time mother, a part-time teacher. They owned their own home and never had more money in the bank. Elizabeth realized at that moment that the Lord had answered the prayers she spoken on that desolate Texas highway. She thanked God that she would have a happy normal family and life after all.

When Elizabeth stood at the entrance to her church, with her father at her side, it was only a month after her annulment had come through. The parish priest informed her that she may marry in the church, with the church's blessings. The wedding party that turned to watch her walk down the aisle with her father amounted to just more than 20 people, but all that mattered is that they were the most important 20 people in her life. Once the blessing of the marriage was completed, everyone filed out to head to the reception. Elizabeth and Carson saw a tall, well-dressed man standing at the entrance. He reached out and shook Carson's hand, kissed Elizabeth on the cheek and said: "Both of you will be together for the rest of your lives. Bless you." And with that he walked out the door. Later, at the reception Elizabeth had asked around if he was with the church. No one seemed to remember anyone like him being there. The priest said: "It was probably your guardian angel."

* * *

"Here. Have a Piña Colada," Carson said as he handed Elizabeth a frosty glass when she arrived home.

"Okay…what is it Carson?"

"What do you mean? I know you like Piña Coladas, that's all."

"You're up to something…"

"Miami."

"To vacation?"

Carson didn't answer.

"To live?"

"I'll be heading the entire South-East Region."

"Another move? You gotta be kidding me."

"Come on, it'll be fun. What can be more fun than living at The Love Boat's home port?"

"Isn't the love boat's home port Los Ange…?" Jacob attempted to correct.

"Same thing." Seeing Elizabeth's frustration. "What the heck are you complaining about? I got you the ocean back, didn't I?"

Elizabeth did miss the ocean. Lakes just aren't the same…especially when they are frozen half the year.

"Our office is in downtown Miami. We can find a place along the beach in between Miami and Fort Lauderdale."

"Oh, boy. Here we go again."

Carson's golf game improved by leaps and bounds. Jacob discovered team sports at a Catholic school and Elizabeth continued teaching part time. Miami was approaching their two-year expiration date for places to live and Elizabeth cautiously kept an eye on Carson for any indication of impending surprise move announcements. Rather, one evening she found him angry and grumbling to himself.

"…in this day n' age…sons of…."

"Carson. What's the matter?" Elizabeth asked.

Carson looked over at Jacob who was doing his homework at the kitchen table and shook his head. Later that evening, when Jacob was in bed he responded.

"We're trying to transfer an engineer from our Miami office to Biloxi Mississippi. Business is set to explode down there, and…" Carson looked visibly perturbed.

"And?" Biloxi. She'd heard the name, but prayed it wouldn't be their next move.

"Well, it's in an exclusive new resort area."

"And?" She thought she sensed Carson winding up for his "let's move again" pitch.

"And...well, the guy has a wife and two kids. And they can't...uh, no one will rent a place to them to live."

"Well, why on earth not?"

Carson looked Elizabeth straight in the eye: "Because they're a black family."

"I need your help again," Elizabeth explained to the cigar-smoking gangster over the phone. "Do you have any developments in the Biloxi area? Specifically, at that new resort area they're building off Highway 67?"

"Yeah, we got something down there. We've moved upscale from trailer parks a long time ago. We're doing some condo units down there. Some *friends* might be bringing in casinos."

"Perfect. We have a problem. My husband's company is trying to relocate an employee...he's working on the golf courses and resorts there or something. But no one will rent an apartment or condo to him."

"What do you mean, nobody will rent to them? Do they have bad credit? What's the..."

"They're a black family."

The phone went silent.

"Oh, come on! Not you too?"

"No, no. I've got no problem with the blacks, you understand. Their money is as green as anybody's. It just that..."

"What?"

"It could...you know, be bad for business."

"It is almost 1980, for goodness sake! You just can't let this happen."

"Yeah, but back east, or out west, or up north. You're talking down in Mississippi, Liz. Things are different down there."

Over the next 15 minutes, Elizabeth applied every ounce of her sales experience, technique and persistence to make an impassioned plea to the cigar-smoking gangster to intervene on behalf of the family.

"You know my dad played with some of the jazz greats…many of them in your clubs too."

There was a pause in the conversation. She had launched everything she had at him. She anxiously awaited his reply.

"If they qualify financially, I'll make sure they get a fair shot."

CHAPTER 4

Elizabeth and Jacob returned from school to find Carson puffing on his pipe over irrigation blueprints that he had sprawled over the dining room table.

"Ready to move again?" Carson asked without looking up.

"What's it this time? Fantasy Island?" Elizabeth quipped.

"Close. It's an island." Carson looked up, smiled with a broad, cat-that-caught-the-canary smile. "Try London, England." With a British accent: "Ipswich, actually."

"And where the heck is Ipswich?"

"Near London."

"Out of the country?" Elizabeth set down the shopping bag on the counter and pulled her hair back. "Oh, I don't know, Carson. That's a big step."

"They speak English over there, you know."

"Well, of course they do, Carson."

"If we move there, maybe Jacob will grow up with a British accent. Wouldn't you like that, son?"

"Cool ! Am I'm going to start talking like Obi-Wan Kenobi?"

"Now hang on," both Carson and Jacob looked at her anxiously as she paused to collect her thoughts. "I've got to talk to my Aunt Estelle about this."

Estelle now spent her winters in Miami. She didn't like the place much, she preferred Corpus Christi, but that's where all her New York City friends were. It was about to get unpleasantly warm in Miami and she was preparing to fly back north for the summer.

"Sweetheart! How's my girl?" Estelle grabbed Elizabeth's elbow the moment she opened her condo door. "Come on, we're heading to the beach."

"So, London, England, huh?" Estelle said as she looked the male server up and down while he placed their drinks on the Miami restaurant's seaside veranda table.

"Ipswich, or some such place."

"It's not too far from London, dear."

"I know. But out of the country? We don't even have passports."

"I was there during the war. I was reporter, you know. A war correspondent for Stars and Stripes." There wasn't a conversation that Elizabeth had with Aunt Estelle where she didn't casually reveal yet another career that she'd had during her illustrious life. "It wasn't a pleasant time to be there, of course, during that God-awful war. But I'm sure its lovely now." She wrestled her hair back from the breeze and stared at the ocean horizon. "The British are a lovely people. And if you can engage with higher society there, their true culture, all the better. I was based most of the time at a military airfield in the middle of nowhere, a place called Grafton Underwood."

"It's a big promotion for Carson," Elizabeth sighed. "It's the head office of his company. I don't want to deny him that."

"My dear, I've delighted in watching you and Carson pull yourselves up these past years. With each move, you've grown. But you are so far from fulfilling your full potential. I know you can't see that right now, but I do. It's as clear as day."

Estelle was so in tune with Elizabeth's emotions, it sometimes made her uncomfortable.

"Go to England, dear."

* * *

"What is the purpose of your visit?" the British immigration officer said while reaching for Elizabeth and Carson's passports.

"I'm here for work." Carson paused. "Oh, and she's my wife." The immigration officer grinned slightly when he caught Elizabeth scowling at Carson and Carson's shrugging.

"May I see your work permit then, sir."

Carson hurriedly pulled it from his breast pocket and handed it to the immigration officer, realizing that he probably should have given it together with his passport. But Carson was new at this sort of thing.

"Ah, yes. Leith Sports & Leisure Engineering. I've heard of them. They're up there in…Ipswich, is that correct?"

"That's right. We build golf courses, resorts. Things of that nature. I'm one of their irrigation engineers. I've been reassigned to the head office for a while."

"Right, I see." The officer grabbed a large mechanical stamp, imprinted entry stamps into Elizabeth, Carson and Jacob's passports and handed them back to them. A pleasant smile broke out on his face: "It's a lovely area up there. A very nice part of England. Not too far from the sea. It's a good two hours by car from here at Heathrow Airport."

"Why thank you," Elizabeth replied, returning a pleasant smile of her own.

The immigration officer closed the conversation with a nod and gestured for the next person in line to come forward.

They followed the signs to baggage claim. "Well, he was awfully nice. I thought those guys weren't supposed to smile or anything like that," Carson said.

"That's the Palace Guard, you big dummy!" Elizabeth said through a laugh.

"Oh. Yeah, right." Carson pulled a cheeky grin.

A skinny woman peering through large tortoise shell glasses under a firmly sprayed Margaret Thatcher hairdo was holding a *Leith Sports & Leisure* placard bearing the hand-written names: *Mr. and Mrs. Carson Jordon.* Carson nudged Elizabeth with his elbow, pointed at the sign and fluttered his eyebrows as if to say: *Look! I'm a big shot now*. Elizabeth rolled her eyes.

She was standing next to the baggage carousel that had just begun disgorging their flight's luggage out from its subterranean hole in its center and, though it was still August, the woman wore a sweater and wool skirt— obviously dressed for the London summers. Elizabeth made note: they would not be suffering the Miami Beach heat anymore and made a mental note to pull her shawl from her luggage before leaving the airport.

The woman reached out her hand as she walked over to them. "Mr. Jordon. How do you do. I'm Agnes McPherson, your executive assistant. I recognize you from your photos. We spoke by phone."

"Uh, you can call me Carson," he said, blushing.

"And this must be Elizabeth and Jacob. It's a pleasure to meet you."

While Carson and Mrs. McPherson exchanged pleasantries and plans, Elizabeth and Jacob studied the baggage area. There was all manner of people milling around them. Japanese business men in suits. Tall, slender well-dressed Englishmen. And several bearded men in some kind of Middle Eastern-looking garb were standing and talking—behind them ghostly black figures, presumably their wives, covered from head to toe in black robes. Even their faces were covered. Not even their hands or feet could be seen. Elizabeth had seen this kind of thing in National Geographic magazines, but never in person. Somewhat uncomfortable at the prospect of a woman being forced to go out in public like that, she tried not to stare.

"The driver should arrive momentarily. If you'll point out your luggage to him, he will collect them and we'll be off."

Two days later the realtor spoke into the rear-view mirror as she drove Elizabeth, Carson and Jacob along the A12, winding along the outskirts of Ipswich. "You look like an internationally well-traveled family to me..." Elizabeth and Carson looked at each other and smiled. "...are you up for an adventure?"

So far, they had seen two options. One was a two-story red brick townhome in the City of Ipswich that was walking distance from the main international school. The other a furnished apartment in a glass and steel building in a newer district on the outskirts. The realtor explained that these two types of accommodations accounted for nearly everything she had left to show them. Either one would have been acceptable to Elizabeth and Carson, but they were curious about this new option she was hinting at.

"It is an authentic English countryside experience. It's the hamlet of Woodbridge." Jacob's nose was pressed against the rear door window. He was having the time of his life. "The Woodbridge Middle School is very international for such a small English town. But it is still quintessentially British," she said with pride. "It's just up the road from your offices…a few miles or so."

"Is there a Catholic church in town?"

"Yes, I believe St. Mary's Church, Woodbridge is Catholic."

Carson and Elizabeth looked at each other. "Yeah, sure," said Carson. "Let's have a look."

The realtor stopped at a local petrol station to make a phone call, then returned to the car. "We're in luck. It's still available and open for a showing right now. And it's within your housing allowance budget, of course." Back on the road, she explained that a Leith Sports & Leisure family had been letting it for the past several years, but were recently relocated to their South African office."

"Woodbridge. Is that where the Avebury Golf Center is?"

"Yes, just adjacent to the Avebury Estate. Here we are…" she said with a song in her voice. "We've arrived." She turned to drive through an open weathered wooden gate. The flora on the grounds of the estate were expansive and well coiffured, but kept cozy and tasteful by old mature trees that stood the grounds like sentries. Strategically placed, and cut back over decades, their overall height was deliberately limited so as not to impose on the various buildings that composed the estate.

"Wow! Cool! We're going to live in a castle!" Jacob's eyes lit up when they passed the main home of the estate.

"I'm afraid not, master Jacob. The family that owns this estate still lives there in the main house." It was magnificent and at the same time a humble three-story mansion: its recessed position beside the gravel road winding through the estate made it somehow seem less pretentious. Still, there were no fewer than ten chimneys which rose above its slate roof: some of them with their brick laid in exotic twisted pattern. From what could be seen from the road, there were six roof peaks along its brick and glass facade: half red with brick, half green with the ivy that covered it.

The relator explained that the Avebury family had been there since the 16th Century. Recently, they began to lease the secondary buildings, and occasionally their main hall for events—mostly diplomatic ones, at the request of the state. "We'll be looking at the grandmother's quarters, dear," she explained to Jacob.

After driving back around the main house, which was equally magnificent and understated behind as it was in front, they found a one story building that was connected to the main house by a gravel path. "Here we are." She pulled into a parking spot next to the building. The brick matched the house, but the roof was Spanish tile that was about 30% covered with moss. A slight whiff of dairy farm became apparent as they exited the vehicle. "They raise cattle and horses here," the realtor smiled. "It is an authentic English countryside experience."

A tour of the house revealed plumbing that was in sore need of updating, there were no screens on any of the windows, but other than that, it was perfect.

"We'll take it."

* * *

Jacob had virtually the entire summer free to explore the estate and its formal gardens, tennis lawn court, meadows, creeks, stables and woodlands—his new playground. Unfortunately, he wasn't able to make too many friends until school began in the fall, but at least he seemed happy.

Carson was immediately absorbed in work and, with the boys keeping themselves busy, Elizabeth found herself with idle time on her hands. That just wouldn't do. She accepted an invitation to join the St. Mary's Church, Woodbridge Parish Council. Since, through her own experience with annulment Elizabeth had become the resident expert on the subject, she started working with the local ministry to help women with going through the process. She would take their testimony and prepare it for presentation to the Church to begin proceedings. When school began, she joined Woodbridge Middle School's Parent Teacher Organization and volunteered for any assignment she could get her hands on. One, fund raising through a local thrift shop, helped raise money for extracurricular activities for the school's students. And, all the while, when needed to play *executive wife* for Carson, she eagerly played this supportive role.

One lovely fall day there was a knock at the door. A trim woman with an elegant French twist hairstyle, who appeared to be in her early sixties was at her front door. "How do you do? You must be Elizabeth Jordon," she said in high English. "I'm Theresa Avebury," she reached out her hand to shake it in a surprisingly casual fashion.

Elizabeth was made quite nervous by the sudden, unexpected encounter. She was informed that Lady Avebury was spending her summer holiday at her family's modest villa on the Portuguese Algarve coast. It made sense that, now the season being over, she'd returned. Elizabeth would later learn that Lady Avebury made a point of personally meeting and getting to know all those who leased properties on her estate. "I was just preparing to have some of your wonderful English tea. Would you join me please?" Elizabeth offered.

The ladies settled at the small, two-person tea table that was set up just outside. It was a cool and sunny fall day, and the grounds of the estate never looked prettier. Lady Avebury was dressed in knee-high black leather riding boots, tight tan pants, a high-collared white blouse cloaked by a dark brown tweed jacket that went down to the mid-thigh. Although she appeared prepared to go riding, no horse was in sight. With the main house and rolling hills of the estate back-dropping Lady Avebury, Elizabeth was enraptured by where her life had led her.

"My husband, God rest his soul, was American you know," she offered, as she stirred her tea. "We met during the war. He was one of the officers who resided here when our house was pressed into service." She explained that after the war they would split their time between the Avebury Estate and her husband's home in McLean, Virginia. He passed away in 1976. "It wasn't unusual for an English woman to marry an American like that," she said. "But I did not have the blessing of my family. They wanted me to marry into British society."

"I know what that feels like," Elizabeth shared. "I didn't have the blessing of my family for my first marriage either. The problem is, they were right. But I did have their blessing for my marriage to Carson."

"My husband sustained a long illness and I was away from Avebury Estate for nearly 2 years."

She'd returned a widow, coming back to find things in shambles—financially. Her father had taken possession of the house from his father who passed away in the 1950s. And with her father's passing in 1977 it was handed down to her. "That's when things started going off the rails, my dear. You wouldn't know it to look at us, but our family has been quite cash-strapped." Elizabeth learned that successive socialist governments since the end of the war imposed massive wealth taxes, but the inheritance tax was the most devastating to families like hers. "We're the fortunate ones," Lady Avebury said. "Others have had to sell off their estates piece by piece, until they were entirely gone. But by the grace of God ours has managed to remain intact. Though I do fear for the next generation."

Elizabeth set aside her astonishment that someone with an estate like hers could have money problems—same as she had all her life. But sharing some of her struggles with money, and compassion for the Avebury family's trials earned her a smile of gratitude from Lady Avebury.

Lady Avebury changed the subject. "So, how do you like your accommodations? Are you settling in alright?"

"No, no. Everything is fine," Elizabeth said, pouring more tea for Lady Avebury.

She noticed Lady Avebury studying her closely. "There must be something. Please, don't be bashful."

"Well…" For some reason Elizabeth felt quite at ease now with Lady Avebury. "I don't mean to offend but, I do have a suggestion." Lady Avebury perked up to listen carefully. "The plumbing really needs updating. If you buy the materials, we'd be happy to do the installation ourselves."

Lady Avebury seemed pleasantly surprised. "Do you know anything about plumbing, my dear?"

"I don't. But my husband designs and builds multimillion dollar irrigation systems for golf courses and resorts. I think he can handle installing a few pipes and single spigot sinks."

"I see. Very well then. Have your husband draw up the plans. Is there anything else?"

"Well, there is the issue of no screens for the windows. I don't see them on any of the buildings around here. Now I don't mind the occasional smell of cattle coming through my windows: I am a hardscrabble Texas girl, after all. But I don't like the flies coming in."

Lady Avebury's smile betrayed her becoming smitten with Elizabeth. "Well aren't you the industrious one? I'll put you in touch with some local craftsmen in Woodbridge who can help build them for you."

* * *

Jacob screamed as he ran from his room in a panic. "I saw a ghost! I saw a ghost! It was in my room!"

"Well it's about time that ghost showed up. It's been almost two years and we've never seen it." Carson said, keeping his pipe clenched in his teeth.

"What? You knew about this? And you moved us in here anyway?" Jacob was livid.

"Oh Carson. Don't fill the boy's head with nonsense," Elizabeth said as she stacked dishes into their new dishwasher.

"Alright, fine. Don't believe me. But some of the people at work told me that this house we're living in is haunted. The grandmother died from being thrown from a horse." Carson sat up and removed his pipe from his mouth and said excitedly: "Say, Jacob, was the ghost a woman and was she dressed for riding?"

"All I saw was a face, made of…like, steam, in my window, except my window was open."

"As long as she doesn't damage my screens she can stay, Jacob!" Elizabeth shouted from the kitchen. "I had each of those custom made in Woodbridge—they cost Lady Avebury a small fortune." Elizabeth was quite proud of her screens, and the fact that others had liked what she did and that screens were popping up all over the estate and nearby town…at the pub, the elementary and middle schools—even some of the other houses. Thanks to Elizabeth, the Jordon family had become a fixture in Woodbridge. In addition to everything else Elizabeth had on her plate, she was a volunteer arts & crafts teacher and so, got to know many families. But it was her lead role in publishing the bi-monthly Woodbridge Magazine where she applied her selling skills to selling advertising locally, that she became known to every business within reasonable driving distance. And in England—a nation of shopkeepers—that meant she'd gotten to know just about everyone in Woodbridge. Jordon blossomed into early teenage and the locals practically adopted him. Carson received yet another promotion.

But no one did more than Lady Avebury to ingratiate Elizabeth into local British society.

Taking her under her wing, they regularly attended social events and various society meetings— two of Elizabeth's favorites being the National Flower Arranging Society and the Women's Institute. Elizabeth became a fixture at such gatherings and became their charming and feisty little lady from Texas: their modern-day, unsinkable Molly Brown.

*　*　*

"Where the heck are my sunglasses!" Elizabeth shouted loud enough for Carson and Jacob to hear on the other side of the house. "One of the few sunny days of the year here and I can't find them. I always keep them right here, on top of the key caddy…"

"The ghost must have moved them, mum" Jacob's muffled voice came from his bedroom.

"Aw, come on," Elizabeth whispered under her breath to the ghost. "Don't do this to me again…no games today, please. This is a very important day for me."

It was a day that was simply beyond Elizabeth's imagination, a mere two years earlier: picking up Aunt Estelle at Heathrow Airport, driving her through London to Woodbridge. Though she was now approaching 70 years old, she still travelled as well as any 20-year-old. Elizabeth knew that the two of them would have the time of their lives during her ten-day holiday in England. Carson would be travelling for business most of the week and it was mid-school year so Jacob wouldn't be able to join them for their 'round Britain tour.

It started with a train journey to Inverness, Scotland and a stay at the Columba Hotel. Followed by another day in Scotland, in Edinburgh, where a friend had arranged for them to sit in the observer's gallery during a session of the Scottish Parliament. And, a quick stop in York on the way back to Woodbridge. Elizabeth planned a surprise destination for Aunt Estelle, one that would require a long drive through the English countryside.

"Does any of this look familiar?" Elizabeth said, tooling along one-lane side roads and seeing the first sign for Kettering. Aunt Estelle was stunned into silence: something that Elizabeth had never seen from her before in all the years she knew her. A few miles later, when they reached Grafton Underwood and Elizabeth pulled off the road to stop next to an old aircraft control tower, Estelle took a deep breath and put her hand over her mouth. She looked over at Elizabeth and held her hand. She didn't need to speak. Her tearful eyes said "thank you" all by themselves. They spent part of the afternoon walking amongst barracks and other buildings of the former USAAF Station 106, or what was left of them after time had taken its toll.

Aunt Estelle led Elizabeth by the hand, narrating the story of her time spent there during the war. She spoke of happy times: "We yanks used to call this place Grafton *Undermud*...because it rained all the time and we were constantly dealing with the mud. The Brits just called it...England," she said with a laugh. And the unhappy times: "So many young lives cut short," she shook her head. "You know more boys died in the air war over Europe than Marines in the Pacific?"

After a few more days wandering through Woodbridge shops and having high tea with Lady Avebury in her estate's old Rectory, Elizabeth was ready to spring one more surprise on Aunt Estelle. It was one that would be beyond even *her* imagination. The two of them took the train into London for a couple days of sight-seeing and shopping before Aunt Estelle left England. On their way to a museum, Elizabeth instructed their cab driver to stop at a back entrance to Buckingham

Palace, one with a sign out front that read: "The Royal Mews."

"Elizabeth…" Aunt Estelle said warily. "…what are we doing here?"

They were met by Lady Avebury's cousin who was in charge of The Royal Mews. Moments later, they were standing before The Gold State Coach.

"Oh, my God. This isn't…" Aunt Estelle put her arm around Elizabeth's shoulder. "Is this the carriage that they use for coronations and such?"

"None other." Elizabeth was smiling from ear to ear.

"We're not supposed to do this…" Lady Avebury's cousin said. "…but Lady Avebury suggested that you might like to sit inside?"

Surrounded by gold and seated upon the finest upholstery, all meant for royalty, Aunt Estelle paused to take in the grandeur and gravitas of the moment. She took Elizabeth's hand: "So dear, I see you've come a long way from that day you called me to declare that you would forever be a 23-year-old, divorced Catholic girl with a toddler, no visible means of support, and abandoned by her ex-husband." She gave Elizabeth a deep hug finishing with a heart-felt smile that made her look absolutely regal and appropriate for the setting: "So, now what do you have to say for yourself?"

* * *

"Do you think that you could do radio?" Lady Avebury asked Elizabeth, as if on a whim.

"Radio?"

"Elizabeth…" Lady Avebury paused to close the door to the Garden Room of her mansion where she and

Elizabeth were privately having high tea. "Did I ever mention what my husband did for a living?"

"No. Just that he was an American military officer who lived in McLean Virginia," sensing the seriousness of Lady Avebury's tone, she set down her tea cup and prepared to listen intently.

"He was with the OSS during the war, you see…the precursor to the Central Intelligence Agency."

Elizabeth became nervous for some reason, but she didn't know why. A week earlier she had met a CIA Communications Liaison Officer stationed in London at one of Lady Avebury's events, but it was such a casual meeting that Elizabeth thought nothing of it. We have people like that all over the world, she reasoned. There was nothing unusual about that. But now, she sensed there might be more to it than that.

"When our estate was pressed into war, being on the coast, we were part of *Chain Home*, a wall of radar receivers whose job it was to pinpoint and report incoming enemy aircraft. Our home served as headquarters for the American OSS stationed in the region, which of course is where I met my husband." Lady Avebury smiled at whatever look Elizabeth now had on her face, stood, took her hand and led her up the stairs to a study off of the master bedroom. She unlocked the door. "What you are about to see is my private collection of war-time spy-craft: one of the largest private collections in existence."

Lady Avebury walked Elizabeth through her collection, educating her on each piece of memorabilia: from button hole cameras and fake travel documents to a picture of Winston Churchill at the foot of Avebury House's stairs and a framed hand-written thank you note from Virginia Hall.

"Virginia Hall. Do you know who she was, dear?" Elizabeth didn't. "She was an American who was living in Europe at the time the war broke out. She joined British intelligence and went clandestine on the European continent for much of the war. She would have been executed the moment she was discovered. But she went on to join the OSS and become one the most successful women spies of the war." Lady Avebury picked up the wood and glass frame that encased Virginia Hall's note. "She was our guest here on numerous occasions. She was a hero in our circles and I absolutely idolized her," she admitted, blushing while checking the tightness of her French twist hairdo. Composing herself: "Shall we return to our tea?"

Elizabeth was dumbfounded. She could now practically smell the gravity of the history that surrounded her as they made their way down the stairs to the Garden Room. Why had Lady Avebury chosen now to reveal all of this to her? Why was she revealing any of it to her at all?

Lady Avebury poured the tea. "I'm going to come right to the point, Elizabeth. I see tremendous potential in you, dear. The fact of the matter is, that both my husband and I were in the OSS, and later the CIA. I'm still active and the new Reagan Administration has some very different ideas about how to deal with the Soviet threat. One of which, I'm convinced you'd be perfect for."

The bottom of Elizabeth's stomach dropped out and she wanted to pinch herself. Was this really happening? Perhaps it was a practical joke, something Carson had dreamed up—and at any moment he would come from behind the curtains laughing at how she fell for the intrigue. It would be just like him…but not Lady Avebury. Surely, she wouldn't be party to such a childish plot.

"You are perfect for the role we are looking for: the unassuming expat spouse…medium height, medium build, you are the right age. In a word: inconspicuous." She explained that they needed to establish a steady stream of communication with a new generation of agents on the other side of the Iron Curtain. "We need someone to broadcast coded messages that the Soviet Block would never suspect. The BBC, Radio Free America they are all monitored day and night. And we have to broadcast through the BBC: it is the only station that uses enough power to reach deep into the Soviet Union." New computer technology rapidly picked up patterns and effectively decodes broadcasts. The only solution was to hide coded messages where they least suspect it. "And, an Elizabeth Jordon radio show would be just the right hiding place."

"Lady Avebury, Theresa, you know I've never done anything like this before. What makes you think I am even capable of this?"

"You're a clever girl. I've been watching you now for a couple years and I became convinced a long time ago that you have what it takes. I was just waiting for the right assignment for you."

So, now what do I have to say for myself? What would Aunt Estelle think of her if she declined? Estelle would of course leap at the chance, wouldn't think twice about it, then nonchalantly mention it in passing in conversation 20 years later. "*Yes. And, when I was a spy, I…*" Just another one of the mysterious and wonderful things she did during her life.

"You would create a show and broadcast from our studio down in Chelmsford." Lady Avebury pressed on. "It's about 50 miles along the A12, between here and London. We need one show a week, to start: 11 to 11:30 PM on Saturdays."

Elizabeth hesitated. "I'll need to discuss this with Carson and Jacob...my Aunt Estelle...I need time to think about this."

Lady Avebury set down her tea cup and took both of Elizabeth's hands in hers. "My dear, you can't tell anybody that we've had this conversation. And if you decide to do this, you won't be able to tell anyone either. Ever. Not even your husband."

*   *   *

The dress rehearsals went well. Elizabeth had this thing down—her first show anyway. While she waited for the top of the hour to roll around, she pondered the symbolism of doing her first radio show from Chelmsford: appropriate for her launching her radio show since Chelmsford itself was the birthplace of radio. Again, she could practically smell the history that surrounded her.

Her mind snapped back into sharp focus when the news presenter coming through her headphones began: "...and now a new show we're convinced you'll all enjoy: some local flavor from just up the path in Woodbridge. She's an American expatriate who founded and publishes the popular and nationally read *Woodbridge Magazine*..." Elizabeth watched the studio producer count down from five with his fingers...four...three... "...the BBC is proud to present

Elizabeth Bromwell's: *Let's Just Talk* radio." Elizabeth thought her maiden name sounded more interesting than her married name.

"Well, good evening Britain. This is Elizabeth Bromwell of *Let's Just Talk...*"

It was the last segment of her first show and time to answer letters to the editor from her magazine subscribers: a kind of Dear Abby regular segment, except the subject matter was limited to English country living. Somewhere contained within one of the questions (or her scripted answers) was the coded message that would be monitored by agents huddled somewhere in the shadows on other side of the Iron Curtain. Her hands shook the script so badly that she needed to hold her jacket's lapels to steady it enough for reading. Covert operatives somewhere behind the curtain would be hanging on her every word now. What if what she read got someone imprisoned? Or killed? Or started a war or something? This was the real deal! She imagined a young Aunt Estelle at Grafton Underwood USAAF Station 106 searching the sky for crippled bombers returning full of injured men, then took a deep breath and read each question through without fail—followed by her answers. Lady Avebury was beaming and nodding approvingly. She gave Elizabeth a thumbs-up through the studio glass.

* * *

"Spain," was the first word out of Carson's mouth when he arrived home.

"What's that, dear?" Elizabeth said innocently, without looking up from her kitchen work.

"Madrid." Was the next word.

Elizabeth smiled broadly: "For holiday or to live?"

"To live," he said slightly perturbed.

"What's wrong with Spain? We've had a couple of lovely holidays there over the past four years here."

"What's wrong? Is this a promotion or a demotion? We have very little going on there. We don't even have a decent sales office. It will take a year, maybe two just to get some things going."

"Well, isn't that what you do dear," again, not looking up.

"It's what I've done. But I was hoping we'd be returning to The States after England. A corporate role in San Diego. Not another start-up field operation." He sighed as he set down his briefcase and blueprint tubes. "But it comes from the very top, so someone must think highly of me there."

"Come on, it'll be fun," Elizabeth struggled to keep a straight face. "Jacob can learn Spanish; would you like that son?"

Elizabeth was needed in Spain. The steady traffic of people coming out from behind the Iron Curtain had reversed: many were now returning to work from within. Elizabeth's international relocation company was barely four months old. They'd done two test runs relocating dissidents back behind the Iron Curtain. Southern Europe was deemed a better location than England for this kind of operation and Elizabeth's assignment was to now move to Madrid and fully open her international relocation company. Lady Avebury herself had spoken to the Chairman of Leith Sports & Leisure Engineering, plc., who was often her golf partner on a neighboring course. Carson had no idea that she had arranged for

Carson's timely transfer to Madrid.

Carson just shook his head. "Olé!" he chimed to Jacob as he used his Burberry topcoat as a cape while Jacob attacked it with his outstretched index fingers on his head.

After movers took the last of their possessions out the front door Elizabeth alone did the final walk through the house—to make sure nothing was missed. She stopped and stood in the middle of the house. "Whoever you are, ghost, thank you for sharing your home with us. It was a wonderful four years." A tear welled up in Elizabeth's eye. "I hope the next family finds as much joy and happiness here as we did." Composing herself Elizabeth started toward the door and hung her set of house keys on the key caddy. When she reached for the door knob she suddenly had a premonition. Elizabeth turned, returned to her bedroom. She looked at the nightstand with the stuck drawer. Depending on the time of the year, and the resulting relative humidity, the drawer would sometimes open, but most often remained frozen shut. Therefore, they hadn't used it since the first weeks after they first moved in. Elizabeth slid the drawer open.

Her sunglasses were inside.

CHAPTER 5

"*Es perfecto*," "it's perfect," Elizabeth told the realtor in her high-school Spanish. "*lo tomaré*," "I'll take it." There was absolutely nothing out of the ordinary with the 42 square meter (453 square foot), store-front office off of Madrid's Calle de Sagasta Street that Elizabeth was renting for her Bromwell Relocation Services. It was unassuming—just like the American expat spouse who ran it.

The Madrid American International School eagerly accepted Jacob's transcripts from Woodbridge's Farlingaye High School. Jacob didn't complain about anything after coming home from his first day of school, which for a mid-teens expat brat was an indication of a successful transfer. Carson's office was within walking distance of Bromwell Relocation's new office downtown, so it was possible for the two of them to easily come in and out of the city together—and even have lunch together from time to time.

Being downtown with Carson brought her some degree of comfort: if they were going to get blown up, at least she and Carson would be blown up together. While having lunch in a street-side café with the General Manager of Leith Sports & Leisure Spain, who was showing them around Madrid their first weekend there, a bomb went off on the next street over. The blast was so powerful, bits of broken glass and a small amount of other debris had passed over the five-story building and lightly sprinkled their table's umbrella. "It's those Basque separatists, I'm afraid. One of their car bombs killed 21 just last week..." The General Manager awkwardly stretched a smile. "Yes, we have a little thing going on here called the Spanish Dirty War. You never get used to it, but you'll learn to live with it." Elizabeth knew about the civil war before she agreed to the Madrid assignment. Still, it was quite different reading about terrorist attacks in Madrid, than actually being in one. She agreed to the assignment, she had no excuse. She could see that Carson was of the same mind. Nothing to do but bravely solider on.

Home in Madrid was a large and luxurious and high-security house in a neighborhood that backed up to the fairways of Golf La Moraleja, Campa 2 north of city center. Entertainment being a big part of the sales process in Spain, the house was for entertaining influential government officials as much as it was a residence for the Jordons. Since moving in three months earlier, Elizabeth was able to convert one of the rooms to a radio studio where she could continue her radio show, which now dealt more with expatriate community living than English country lifestyle—which she was no longer privy to.

The CIA maintained a working office in the lower floors of a nearby mansion and for their first three months in Madrid, Elizabeth received daily covert tactics and methods training there while Carson was at work and Jacob in school. To her friends and family, she expertly played the bored expat wife who couldn't get the domestic helper to clean properly. And, complained about the *noblesse oblige* of having to attend three-hour lunches in the latest trendy Madrid restaurants with "the girls" from the expat community. But the time for applying her training was to begin just days after she moved into Bromwell Relocation's new office. And Elizabeth was nervous.

* * *

"I was a German wolf child," the 50-year-old man said to Elizabeth in a perfect American mid-western accent, just over the din of the restaurant. "Do you know what that is?" he asked as he held the plate of paella for Elizabeth to take a serving from.

"No sir. I don't." He was Elizabeth's first assignment through Bromwell Relocation Services. Their lunch followed a morning going through an elaborate procedure for signing over a briefcase filled with various documents. There was his new US Passport, name: Angelo McCloud—a nice Italian-Scottish mongrel American name. Currencies: US Dollar cash and American Express travelers cheques, Spanish Pesetas, West German Deutsche Marks, and East German Marks. And, normal paraphernalia for a 1980's American business man: an address book/organizer with its calendar filled in with events for the rest of the year. An envelope hand-labeled "expense report" that was stuffed with receipts from several countries—matching the dates of entry and exit stamps of corresponding countries in his passport. An American Express charge card. A Montblanc fountain pen. Business cards with Angelo McCloud printed under his import/export company letterhead. And business cards from various companies corresponding to the places he visited stamped in his passport. And of course airline tickets: a used one and boarding pass stub for one Angelo McCloud from Miami to Madrid, days earlier. And new ones: Madrid to Berlin and back to Miami. Once in Berlin he would cross the inner German border to East Berlin. Finally, his week-long reservation in an East German Interhotel, where they would surely routinely rifle through his possessions as they would do his briefcase while crossing the border.

Mr. McCloud took a sip of his wine, savored it for a moment, then turned to Elizabeth. "We were among tens of thousands of German families living in East Prussia—ordered there as part of Hitler's promise of "living space" for his Third Reich. I was only eleven years old, the second oldest of five siblings. After the Russian Red army stopped the German advance, where my father was most likely killed, and began driving toward Germany, we had to abandon our home there. We hoped to rush back west just ahead of them, to Germany and hopefully the allies—the Americans if we could. Everyone knew if we were caught by the Russians, they would kill us…or worse. Or both."

They started out with all the possessions they could load onto horse-drawn carts. "The things that were precious to me as a child then: my toys, my clothes…" He paused, smiled awkwardly and shrugged "…my Hitler Youth uniform and books." But the snow was deep, he explained, and they got stuck on a road through the wilderness. "So we made make-shift sleds for the horses to pull and took only what was essential from the wagons—leaving the rest behind." Then exhaustion and starvation began to set in. He stared blankly. "Someone shot our horse and we all ate its meat. But we could no longer pull the sleds, so we took again only what was now absolutely essential, only what we could carry. And left the rest behind. But the snow. Oh, the snow." It became so deep that every step became a near impossible task—so they left their remaining possessions behind. "All we had were the clothes on our backs and dried strips of horse meat to sustain us. I'm talking about weeks out in the open."

But still they pushed on, across frozen lakes and hills and endless forests. "West. Always West." He had heard grown-ups talking about America, but it was just an abstract concept to him. He didn't believe there was such a place that could coexist with all the misery he and his family were surrounded by. "But then we started dying. Sickness, starvation, exhaustion. There was no way to bury the dead in the frozen ground, so we just left them, a trail of frozen bodies along the side of the road." They had started out with his mother and her five children, but they began to succumb to privation and the elements. "My baby brother died of some kind of sickness, maybe exposure, but my mother couldn't bring herself to lay him by the side of the road like the other bodies." She carried him in her arms for many kilometers until she fell and couldn't get up. She had given her children all her food rations, and became sick and weak. Her legs were cramped and she couldn't move. "We could hear the Russian artillery behind us. We had to keep going." Others began pushing he and his remaining siblings along. "They just told us that we had to keep going. So that is where we left her: my mother and my baby brother, there, by the side of that frozen road. Forever."

He paused to take a deep breath and another sip of his wine. Elizabeth was in shock, her heart palpitating, unable to do anything but look at this man and wonder how it was possible that he was sitting before her that day. He inhaled briskly: "So, we just kept walking. I don't know how long. Many days. And when we ended up in Lithuania? There were thousands of us orphans...I don't know. Five-thousand? Maybe Ten? Scattered all over the countryside in groups of 15 or 20. But none of them were my brothers and sisters. They had been lost along the long march. I was the only one of our family alive."

"Did people there in Lithuania help you?" She pleaded, hoping for some part of humanity to have stepped up and rescued these innocent children.

He laughed, smiled. And shook his head. "No. You see, we were Hitler's swine. No town would accept us. When we would come into town to beg for food they would chase us out like a pack of animals. So we lived in the forest nearby. Spring had come and with the mud we were always dirty, with no way to wash ourselves. And always hungry, so....hungry." He closed his eyes and strained against the memory. Living in the woods, they were called wolf children, because they lived like a pack of wolves in the forest.

"You were out there in the forest for six months? How on earth did you survive?"

"The spring planting season saved us. Lithuanian farmers would feed us one meal for an entire day's work. One meal, one day. We were slave labor to them, but that is how we survived that summer: days in the fields, nights in the forest." He smiled when he told Elizabeth that after the final harvest a woman from town came out to them one day, took them to her house and washed them all. She re-clothed them. "It was the first time I'd worn shoes since the early spring," he nodded and drew a shaky breath. "And then she took us to the rail yard, put us on a freight car and told us to hide." The train was heading to Eastern Germany, where they were taken in by orphanages. "We also worked for our meals there. But at least we had a roof over our heads, hot food in our bellies and toilets under our bums," he said with a smile.

"Oh my…." Elizabeth choked up. "It is an absolute miracle of God that you survived."

"Yes, but I was still a slave in East Germany—not so much a slave of the body anymore, but of the heart and mind. So, what is a 15 year old man, alone in the world, and stuck in East Germany – to do? There was only one thing to do: escape to the west." And he did, all the way to America. He learned English by secretly listening to the BBC. Then escaped from East Germany to Austria. Then from Austria to Canada. And then from Canada to America. "I arrived on my 16th birthday and attended high-school, then college in warm and sunny south Florida, where I've lived ever since."

"I know you can't discuss your mission with me, but why do you want to go back?" Elizabeth was terrified. She even wanted to talk him out of his mission…whatever it was. What if she'd made an error with his documents and the East German Police discovered it? This poor man who'd endured such unspeakable suffering, who overcame such insurmountable odds—and it would be Elizabeth who did something that sent him back into hell? Just the slightest oversight on her part could get this man killed…or worse. Or both!

"Every day, I still see my mother sitting there by the side of the road holding my dead brother. I've had a good life in America up to now. I need to go back and help change things for the people there. I've left too many people behind. There is a growing dissident movement that can help us make real change happen. The Polish Solidarity movement is one. But there are others." He looked deeply into Elizabeth's eyes: "It is time for me to free my people from slavery of the heart and mind."

* * *

"What's the matter dear," Carson asked Elizabeth as they threaded their way through Madrid's traffic on the drive home. "You seem a bit...melancholy." He knew he was using an outdated term, but it seemed to fit the moment.

"Oh, nothing. It's just been a busy first week for the agency. I guess I'm a little tired."

Carson, always the sensitive, caring and thoughtful gentleman: "Do you want to eat out tonight? Save you the trouble of making dinner?"

Elizabeth smiled and put her hand on his. "No, dear. I want to make you and Jacob dinner tonight. I'll be fine."

Elizabeth experimented on her family with a few of the recipes that listeners to her show had mailed in: a Greek dish and two Spanish dishes that her domestic helper had prepped for cooking before she went off duty. Carson and Jacob eagerly enjoyed her dinner as they talked about their respective days. Elizabeth sat there at the dining table that night slowly, quietly eating. What could she say to them about her day? That she was now part of the underground railroad for Eastern Block slaves of the heart and mind? Rather, she just smiled, reached out her hands, squeezed her husband and son's arms, and personally thanked God for all the blessings of her life.

CHAPTER 6

"We'll be back...I don't know...some time," Carson said as he and Jacob flip flopped down the porch stairs of Lady Avebury's villa for the first swim of their week-long holiday on the Portuguese Algarve.

"Please watch yourselves going down those stairs to the beach. They're absolutely treacherous when they get covered with sand," Lady Avebury cautioned.

"Thanks, Aunt Theresa!" Jacob shouted back.

"Oh, they'll be fine, Theresa. Your glass is empty." Elizabeth refreshed Lady Avebury's wine glass.

"Thank you, dear. Are you all settled in?

"Nicely, thank you very much."

They chatted like they were still living on Lady Avebury's estate in England. But now, instead of watching the crows soar over the English countryside, they watched the white gulls hover in the deep blue sky on the steady breeze rising up from the face of the Algarve's trademark red sandstone cliffs.

"You've done such a splendid job with Eastern Europe over the past two years, dear. But things have gotten quite on track there. The agents you've placed have been very effective." She took a long sip of her wine. "The action for the moment is the bloody Russians in Afghanistan. That war seems to have no end to it." She looked Elizabeth straight in the eye—"We need you in Turkey."

Lady Avebury had forewarned Elizabeth that their holiday would involve a discussion about her reassignment. While she was grateful that she and her family would remain on the right side of the cold war's Iron Curtain, hot conflicts involving open warfare naturally scared her.

"We need you to accomplish three things. First: move your radio show closer to the region. Working through the BBC has just simply become too obvious for the current technology, I'm afraid. We need to move to local radio stations, ones within reach of communications with the Afghan resistance to the Soviet occupation forces and other resistance fighters in the region. Second, we need you to get people into theater, just as before—new identities and legitimate relocations—into Pakistan, mostly. Our assets in Pakistan will take it from there. And third, to help us keep our end of the bargain with the Turkish government for their cooperation—establish an underground railroad for Turkic minority VIPs who've been trapped in Afghanistan, for resettlement in Turkey."

"Istanbul is a fascinating city. We've vacationed there. Carson loved it. I know expat families who've raved about the international school there. We'll just have to move Jacob in his senior year, unfortunately. But all these kids know each other across all these international schools anyway."

"I'm sure they do, dear. But I'm afraid that the location of your assignment is Antalya Turkey. And you'll be commuting weekly to Cyprus to do your radio show—our office and studio is in Nicosia."

*   *   *

It wasn't but three days after they'd returned from holiday on the Portuguese Algarve that Carson arrive home from work and gave his one word announcement about their next move.

"Turkey!"

"Sorry, dear, but we're having lamb tonight." Elizabeth sang, barely holding in her knowing grin.

Carson squinted at Elizabeth. "No…the country."

Elizabeth tilted her head from side to side. "Oh, I see. But you loved Istanbul when we…"

"Not Istanbul. Antalya."

"Where the heck is Antalya," Jacob demanded, panicked that his social life would suddenly dwindle to mountain goats and rural tribesman.

"Exactly! Don't worry, you're not going. There's nothing there for you. Not even an International School. You're going to boarding school back in England."

Elizabeth silently cheered, that was one thing she wouldn't have to convince Carson to agree to. But she now studied Jacob's face. He was weighing being with his friends, while still having to spend his final year of high school living with his parents, versus making new friends while on his own in an English boarding school. With a shrug he indicated that he was ready to render his verdict. "Cool."

"Yeah, well I was ready to leave Spain, even for another international assignment if there wasn't anything back in The States…but small-town Turkey?"

"Well, it is on Turkey's south Mediterranean coast. When was the last time we lived on the water anyway, Carson? Miami? I miss the ocean. They have to call it the

Turquoise Coast for a reason, I'm sure it's beautiful."

"How do you know so much about it?" Carson grumbled.

"Uh, hello! I run a relocation company and sometimes travel agency...hello!"

"Oh, yeah."

"Come on..."

"Yeah, yeah, yeah. I know. Come on, it will be fun."

*   *   *

If one had grown up near the sea, and missed it, and needed to be stuck in a smaller town abroad, one could do far worse than Antalya, Turkey. From the 3,200 square foot ocean-view villa that Carson's company had rented for them overlooking the Western Mediterranean sea, they could always count on seeing cruise liners and sailboats plying the deep blue waters. When it came time to enjoy the sea themselves, a short drive brought them down from their lush green neighborhood atop red sandstone cliffs, to Konyaalti's smooth pebbly beaches where the blue Mediterranean made a foundation for the rutty mountain peaks it upheld in the distance off round the bay. And when one had had enough of the beach's hedonistic pleasures, one could indulge their more intellectual delights, say, a seaside lunch in Kaleiça Marina. There, one could marvel at how respectfully ancient walls of long-gone fortifications were integrated into the modern parts of town—and imagine all the lives lived out there over nearly two millennia. Yes, one could do much worse than Antalya. But as Elizabeth and Carson had learned, it is one's attitude that makes a place enjoyable or miserable.

In the beginning, Elizabeth's commute to Cyprus was grueling—involving an entire weekend. After a two hour drive to the ferry port at Alanya, she then took a 4 ½ hour ferry to Girne. All told she spent her first eight hours of her Saturday mornings commuting to Cypress and her final eight hours of Sunday evenings commuting back. And all this to do just one 11:00 PM radio show to read encrypted messages. Fortunately, this dramatically improved after only a few months, when regular flight service commenced between Antalya and Nicosia. This involved only one hour of flight time, where Elizabeth discovered that small planes seemed to unnervingly roll and pitch more than larger jet airliners. The aircraft was brand new though, a 30-passenger Saab 340A. Swedes had established a reputation for automotive safety and time would tell if the same applied to aircraft.

All the while the Cypress Dispute was raging. Talks broke down one day, only to resume the next, and so on. The island was long since militarized and Elizabeth needed to pass through checkpoints, which became as normal in her travel as checking into a hotel. All it took was a little small arms fire to bring down her turboprop. But as happens when risk becomes routine, the mind's panic button turned off as one resigns to fate. She hardly noticed it anymore. The greatest risk she faced in Cyprus was her interactions with people on the ground there.

If there were two peoples who love to disagree over politics it was the Greeks and the Turks. Elizabeth would always wisely sidestep the Cypriot issue of the day being argued over group dinners with the station's staff—half of which were Greek, and the other Turkish. Although there was no shooting war, like in Afghanistan, ethnic and sectarian murders did happen there from time to time.

* * *

Elizabeth watched from her minivan as the afternoon ferry approached the port of Alanya. She was there to pick up three men who'd been smuggled out of Afghanistan. She was there to provide them each new identities and to escort them to Istanbul. By the time the ferry had docked and began disgorging people and cars from its gaping mouth, Elizabeth was standing on the quay holding up a placard. One of three bearded men dressed in wrinkled business suits and carrying brand new suitcases pointed to her. They walked over. Two of them appeared to be in their twenties. Only one spoke English, the older one, who she estimated to be in his forties.

"You are Miss Elizabeth?"

"Yes I am," she offered her hand. No one reached out to shake it. "We're all set. I'll be taking you to your hotel now. And we will be leaving from the airport tomorrow on the 9:00 am flight." The one who spoke English translated. Then all three nodded in unison.

After the four of them piled into her minivan, and began the journey to their hotel, Elizabeth got a cold chill up her spine. The men were very cautious, they didn't even speak to each other. Were they suspicious that she might speak their language? Should she take that as a compliment? The silence and looks they shot back and forth to each other made her feel uncomfortable.

Elizabeth pulled into a rest stop and parked. She needed privacy in a public place. She didn't want to do the handover of documents in the hotel, where her two options would be doing it in a public place with no privacy, such as the hotel's restaurant, or in privacy in one of their hotel rooms—and that wasn't going to happen. "We're going to do the document handover here at this rest stop, okay? We need privacy." She received no objection and swiveled her captain's chair around and began her handover procedure, one by one. Turkish passports, ID's, family photos, the works. They would arrive in Istanbul the next day new men: literally.

Elizabeth had been ogled plenty of times in her life, but nothing like the way the younger two did in the van that day. They looked at her in a way that she found indescribable: a twisted combination of an angry form of hatred and animalistic lust—one that she was certain would derive perverse pleasure in the act of deliberately harming another person. She was convinced that these men were no stranger to violent rape, and that were it not for her present circumstances—helping them escape to Turkey—they surely would have done so right then and there. Brutally so. The older one seemed amused by the whole thing and Elizabeth was certain he held her in distain for simply being a woman. She skillfully concealed the fear that now gripped her deep inside like a clenched fist. She pressed on with doing her job to the letter.

After checking them into the Antalya airport hotel, she bid them good night, turned and walked away. She could hear them laughing behind her back.

The plane ride to Istanbul the next morning revealed them to be lacking experience with modern conveniences. They were truly fish out of water. They struggled with their seat belts. Found the tray tables a mystery and source of amusement. Couldn't figure out the universal symbols of the call button, light and vent above their heads. And one struggled with the bathroom door, leaving it unlocked and having to pull it shut when another passenger attempted to enter unawares. But she didn't hold this against them. If her life had demonstrated anything, it was that what you have does not define who you are. But what you do with what you have, does.

Elizabeth delivered them to agents at the designated place at the Grand Bazaar in Istanbul. As they walked away, speaking with each other and looking back at Elizabeth, she was certain they considered her "the rape that got away." She had no doubt that those men were evil and up to no good. And that it was only a matter of time before they did something to live up to her impression of them. Their evil eyes haunted her on the flight home, uncomfortably waking her each time she dozed off.

Carson was up. "Welcome back. Are you hungry? There are some leftovers. I'll heat them up for you…"

Elizabeth said nothing, set down her bags, made a beeline for Carson, threw her arms around him and began to cry.

"What happened, Liz? Did something happen in Istanbul? Are you alright?"

Elizabeth composed herself, looked at Carson and thanked God for giving him to her. "What's the matter, can't a girl just cry for no reason once in a while?"

CHAPTER 7

Elizabeth and Carson were on the couch watching in amazement the TV broadcast of the last Soviet tanks rolling over a bridge out of Afghanistan. "I never imagined that the Russians would ever give up territory like that. They never let go of something once they have their hands on it," Carson said. Elizabeth nodded.

The phone rang: "The Soviets are out," Lady Avebury told Elizabeth.

"I know, we're watching it right now."

"I'm going to be in Cyprus this Saturday. Plan to stay through Sunday evening."

That Saturday they met at a private table at Lady Avebury's favorite Girne Harbour restaurant. "We've known about the Russian pull-out for months. We don't need you in Turkey anymore."

Elizabeth was relieved. As lovely as the natural environment was, two years in Antalya was more than enough. Elizabeth eagerly awaited her next assignment. Paris perhaps? Florence? The possibilities were endless.

"Problem is, we don't need you back in Europe or the UK anymore. All those seeds you helped plant over the years are beginning to blossom." Lady Avebury explained that while the agency was expecting big things to happen on the other side of the Iron Curtain this coming summer, they expected little demand for her services. "Think…Asia, my dear. That's where the action is. Singapore. From Singapore you will be heading relocation across Asia, for China, Vietnam, Burma, North Korea, Philippines, the lot."

The following week Jacob was home visiting from college, Spring Break. Bored, he had dug through boxes labeled "Jacob's Stuff" in the storage room and found a stack of his old Asterix comic books that he'd grown up on as a kid. He was occupying himself with re-reading them on the sofa when Carson came home from work.

"Singapore." Carson announced, with a sigh.

"Honey, we've heard great things about that place from our expat friends," Elizabeth encouraged.

"What the heck do I know about Asia?"

"What do you need to know? You're a glorified plumber, after all. Stuff rolls down hill and payday is on Friday. What's to know?"

Jacob was still engrossed in his comic books on the sofa when said without losing a beat: "Aren't one of you guys supposed to say: come on, it'll be fun?"

* * *

"Taiwan?" Carson bellowed. "What the heck do you need to go to Taiwan for now? We just got to Singapore. We aren't even over our jet lag yet."

"For my business, of course. There is a lot of business traffic going back and forth between Singapore and Taiwan. And that means relocations." Elizabeth fixed drinks for both of them, then sat down next to Carson. "Besides, Lady Avebury has already made arrangements for me to meet someone she knows there. She's well connected, I guess."

"But I wanted to explore Singapore together with you. High tea at the Raffles Hotel, shopping on Orchard Road...that kind of stuff." Carson pouted.

"I'm only going to be gone for a couple of days. We'll do all those things and more when I get back, okay?"

As Elizabeth stared out the airplane window at the stretch of ocean between Singapore and Taiwan, she heard ringing in her memory, Lady Avebury's suggestion for the first thing to do after she settled her family in Singapore: "You simply must meet Sonya—the very week you arrive. She's an old and dear friend and it would be lovely if you two became acquainted. She's a fascinating person, and there is no one who can teach you more about the people of the region."

Several hours later, Elizabeth was delivered by taxi to the General Chennault Pub. She paused to contemplate Taipei's Jen Ai Road and all manner of vehicles darting in and out of the many small, capillary-like alleyways feeding that major artery. Most of the alleys were choked with cars parked halfway up on their narrow sidewalks. Tangled bunches of wires and cables were strung along the sides of the buildings and across the alleyways like popcorn strings on a Christmas tree.

The Turks and Spaniards have nothing on these people; Elizabeth was in awe of the traffic maelstrom that was playing out before her, in particular the scooters swarming the streets. Dozens of them weaved and flowed forward between the cars and busses queued in long lines at the intersection where she crossed. One scooter had an entire family aboard: a father, a toddler standing on the footplate between the father's legs, and a preteen on the seat sandwiched between her father and mother, who appeared to be well into her third trimester with another child. To Elizabeth's untrained eye there wasn't even organized chaos on the streets, but it seemed to work fine for the people of Taipei.

General Chennault. She recognized the name from school, but forgot the details—something to do with China during the Second World War. She ambled in. The entire bar was decorated with World War II memorabilia and she spent several minutes studying war-buddy photos taken in front of army tents, dented airplane propellers, flying goggles together with a leather helmet, and other artifacts that were hung on the wall. Her attention was caught by a large, ornately carved-wood framed picture of a bald Chinese man with a pleasant smile. He looked familiar, but her school lessons on the war in China were simply too remote.

"He was Chiang Kai-shek, dear," she heard in a Russian-accented voice coming from behind a lattice screen. "He was the president of the Republic of China." Behind the screen, Elizabeth found a mature Western lady sitting at a table, alone, with an open book in one hand and a martini glass in the other. She was a lovely, serene woman with pure white hair pulled into a bun held in place with a pair of black-lacquered chopsticks. Her regal bearing and dress—she wore a black, almost Victorian-style dress, its high lace collar clasped together with a white, oval scrimshaw pendent—brought to mind nineteenth-century portraits of European aristocrats that she'd seen hanging in museums. However, in her high-collared, full-length black dress and grandmotherly white hair, she looked as out of place in the pub as Whistler's mother would have in a speakeasy.

"Madame Chiang, his wife, is a lovely lady. She is from a prominent family in China, the Song family. She has exquisite taste, is a patron of the arts, and quite an accomplished painter herself, as a matter of fact." She paused, contemplating her next comment as a schoolteacher preparing a lesson, then went on to explain that Madam Chiang was a special friend of the United States and had appeared before the U.S. Congress on several occasions, the most famous time being when she asked for American assistance during the war. The woman paused once again to measure her commentary and concluded: "She lives in New York City now. Pity we don't see her back here very often anymore."

Elizabeth was convinced that the woman did not mean her last comment figuratively. By the way she spoke about Chiang Kai-shek and Madame Chiang, it was clear to her that she knew them both personally, but she was too polite to ask.

"How do you do? You must be Elizabeth, Lady Avebury's friend. Please, join me." Her calm, steady smile put Elizabeth at ease. Gesturing around with her martini glass she explained that the things Elizabeth saw on the walls were her and her husband's. "The years that we collected all of this was an important and meaningful time, not only for us but for the rest of the world too. This is history, my dear."

Sonya sipped her drink and sized up Elizabeth. "I'm a White Russian, dear. Do you know what that is? Besides the drink, I mean." Sonya explained that she had never actually been to Russia, but was born and spent her early years in Harbin, China, a city near the Russian border. Her family was part of the Russian aristocracy that fled to escape persecution from the Bolsheviks.

"They were the Russian communist revolutionaries, dear."

She described Harbin as a modern city for its place and time, where many of the more cultured Russians settled after the revolution. As a little girl there, her grandmother would take her to the opera, the ballet, and Russian social clubs.

"Do you speak Chinese too, then?"

"Yes. My nanny taught me," she said. "My mother had grown frail after I was born; she was traumatized by the experience of living as a refugee, poor dear. She was unable to raise me on her own, so my grandmother raised me, as a Russian."

Seeing what must have been a sympathetic look on Elizabeth's face, she made a dismissive, that's-all-in-the-past gesture with her hand. She described her father as a gentle man, a former White Russian general who was completely devoted to his family. The Soviet-Japanese Neutrality Pact made it possible for her family to live in Japanese-occupied China. "They left us Russians alone. At least it kept us out of the labor camps. And it gave me the opportunity to secretly leave Harbin to do my part in the war." She had become a nurse and, through her father's connections with the American military, she went to Kunming, where General Chennault was setting up the Flying Tigers.

"That's where I spent most of the war years," Sonya said, repositioning the aviator's watch that hung loosely around her wrist. "And that's where I met Frank, my husband." She pointed to a framed, eight-by-ten black-and-white photograph of a man in an American uniform that hung on the wall. She described him as a dashing young man with a rare zeal for life. Like the rest of the

Flying Tiger pilots, he was barely out of his teens, and was brazen, and at times reckless and foolhardy. But, she explained, living on life's edge—facing life-and-death battles on an almost daily basis—will do that to a person. "When they weren't flying, they were always in some sort of trouble or another. Frank and I were engaged to be married when I returned to Harbin to rejoin my family."

Her grandmother had cultivated Sonya's love of the stage, and it had been her childhood dream to become a theatrical set designer. "I studied it for a while, but war caught up with us again—that would be the Chinese Civil War, dear, the one between the Chinese Nationalists and the Communists." She and Frank were married in 1949, the same year they arrived in Taiwan. "We lived here, among the U.S. forces and Chinese exiles, until Frank passed away in 1969."

Elizabeth confessed that she'd spent nearly her entire life in the United States and now, most recently, Europe. Other than a week's vacation on Malaysia's Tioman Island, and the Kuala Lumpur airport that they'd arrived through, she had never been in Asia.

Sonya nodded, seeming to acknowledge that Lady Avebury had sent her a beginner. "Elizabeth, you won't be able to understand this culture by comparing it to what you know." Cultures are living things, she said, with their own DNA. "Greek Democracy, the Magna Carta, the Renaissance, the American Revolution, and government of the people were all part of your cultural DNA, not theirs." That Chinese cultural DNA is based on Confucian tradition, one of family hierarchy and the supremacy of the needs of the group over the individual. "For instance, whereas we say, 'Man does not live by bread alone,' the Chinese say, 'Min I Shih Wei T'ien,' or

'For people, food is heaven,' meaning that the essence of what is most important in life is a full belly."

Though Elizabeth may have been ready for more, Sonya caught herself getting lost in the weeds. "In any event," she concluded, "China is an ancient country and it is wise for one to keep an open mind." They spoke of lighter things over the next hour before having lunch brought in.

"It has been so wonderful chatting and dining with you, dear. I see why Lady Avebury has taken a shine to you. You must see some of the local culture while you are here. I have two box seats at the National Theater. There is Chinese opera this evening. Would you care to join me?"

Elizabeth was tickled, but asked: "Is this attire appropriate?" referring to the silk jacket that she was wearing—she'd had it made in Turkey, along with the rest of her outfit.

"Yes. Its lovely, and the opera isn't particularly formal."

The National Theater was within a large, red-columned rectangular building with orange-tiled sloping roofs cascading into upward-sloping eves at the four corners. Each eve was manned by tiny gargoyles. The reception area of the National Theater was floor-to-ceiling classic Chinese in design, with thick red columns that thrust into a complex latticework of multiple layers of interlocking beams that framed hand-painted dragon, phoenix, and other designs. While being led to Sonya's box seats by the stage, Elizabeth was impressed by the wonderfully balanced blend of Chinese-style design and modern theater architecture.

"This was my dream, Elizabeth," Sonya said as she

gestured broadly toward the stage when they took their seats. "Theatrical sets are fleeting, like Indian sand paintings of the American Southwest: They only exist for the purpose and duration of the ceremony, then blow away into so much dust."

Elizabeth wondered out loud what they would see behind the curtain that evening.

"Well, since this is Chinese theater, perhaps just another curtain," Sonya said with a smile, then explained that, unlike Western opera, Chinese opera sets are often little more than a curtain and a few tables and chairs; that the focus tends to be wholly on the actors and their singing and motions. But that sometimes they do experiment with more complex, multidimensional sets.

"We shall see."

Witnessing Chinese opera for the first time, especially with someone who knew it and was patient enough to explain it, was a privilege. It was so foreign, and such an exotic art form to her, that her mind struggled to comprehend it. Though it had singing actors, music, and dance, it wasn't comparable to any European opera, ballet, or London West End theater musical that Elizabeth had ever seen.

She took Sonya's advice to heart and tried not to understand it by the measures of her own experience, but to experience it for what it was. She allowed himself to be overwhelmed by the pageantry of colorful costumes and dramatic face paint; the whipping motion of the incredibly long peacock feathers and the actors' habitual flicking of their ridiculously long sleeves; the actors' melodramatic movements and the falsetto singing, that, like the falsetto-voiced dialogue, fluctuated continuously up and down the scale; all accompanied by whining stringed instruments. The entire performance was hyper-dramatized and segued scene to scene with bizarre sounds made by exotic instruments that pinged, clanged, and rattled in form that would have been unimaginable to her as music before that night.

And Elizabeth's horizons expanded even further than she'd ever imagined.

* * *

By the end of May, Elizabeth had incorporated her relocation company in Singapore and began a multi-city tour across Asia to meet operatives—under cover of making relocation-company partners in each country.

On June 3rd she found herself at a hotel overlooking Tiananmen Square in Beijing. The Beijing Hotel was old and *Soviet-style*, if there was such a thing. As Elizabeth took the elevator up to her room to freshen up, each time the elevator stopped to let people off at their designated floors she noticed a security guard sitting at a desk near the elevators. Sonya had explained that it was routine at Beijing's big city hotels for a security guard to be present on each floor. When she got off on her floor, the security guard reached out and asked for her passport and room key. After making a note in his logbook, he handed Elizabeth back her possessions and waved her down the hall to her room.

Elizabeth was scheduled for a breakfast meeting in the lobby the next morning and so had the evening free. After she'd cleaned up from her travels and put on a fresh set of clothes, and after enjoying a smog-enhanced sunset over Tiananmen Square from her balcony, she left her room under the watchful eye of her floor's security guard. She would take a walk through the city.

As Elizabeth was leaving the hotel she was met by one of the hotel's security officers: "We are advising all our guests to stay in the hotel, for the moment. You are free to go of course, but no one can guarantee your safety."

Perhaps she should have tea at the hotel instead, she thought. Then changed her mind: what the heck kind of spy was she if she just hid in the hotel her entire time in Beijing? She would head to Tiananmen Square, right into the thick of it.

Exiting the hotel and turning right on East Chang An Avenue, she found the first intersection impassable: a group of students and a four-vehicle military troop convoy were in a stand-off, blocking her way. Students were locked arm-in-arm across the intersection, deliberately preventing the convoy from passing through, while others had surrounded the truck and were shouting up to the soldiers in the back, pleading with them to turn around and leave the city.

It appeared that the students were doing their best to explain that they were doing the right thing, that they were peaceful and that the soldiers should not confront them. Elizabeth guessed that the soldiers were likely the sons of peasant farmers rather than the privileged few who had the influence within the government to send their children to university. The soldiers appeared unconvinced and focused on following their orders. Only the convoy commander had stepped down from the cab of the lead truck to speak with the students.

Butterflies were fluttering in Elizabeth's gut. She couldn't imagine any army, let alone the Chinese army, allowing itself to be stopped in such a way for very long.

The expressions on the faces of the convoy commander and his troops clearly suggested to him that the army's patience with the students was wearing thin. Perhaps she should go back to her hotel. Perhaps she should head straight to the airport and get the heck out of Beijing...out of China. Elizabeth decided she'd better leave the scene in any event and, bypassing the intersection, she continued on to Tiananmen Square.

Within the square's expansive area—from her perspective at ground level—there were people for as far as the eye could see. The hum of hundreds of thousands of voices was unlike anything Elizabeth had ever heard or would ever hear again. Passing by the ceremonial flagpole used for official daily flag-raisings, she was drawn toward the thickest masses of people nearer the center of the square. As she struggled through the crowd, Elizabeth could see flashes of a large white figure contrasted against the sea of black hair in front of her. Getting closer, the figure revealed itself to be a makeshift statue of a woman holding a torch with both hands—off to one side and high above her head. It was what Elizabeth recognized from her briefings as the students' Goddess of Democracy. A student noticed Elizabeth in the crowd and walked up to her and said in remarkably good English: "It is just like your Statue of Liberty in America." Though there was some physical resemblance, the intended symbolic meaning was more apparent. What was happening in Tiananmen Square under the watchful gaze of Chairman Mao's massive portrait hanging over the South Gate of the Forbidden City was not lost on Elizabeth. She looked at her watch: time to get back to her hotel.

Using the South Gate of the Forbidden City as a

landmark target through the sea of heads, she began to make her way back through the crowd. When Elizabeth reached the South Gate she discovered that someone had thrown a bottle of black ink or paint, deliberately defacing the portrait of Mao that hung there. Time to go, Elizabeth.

As Elizabeth turned to walk down Chang An Avenue back to her hotel she heard a half-dozen low-pitched thuds behind her at the north end of the square—a cascade of smoke trails arced up over the crowd's heads. Teargas canisters.

Elizabeth's heart pounded in her chest. Time to go, now!

The crowd surged from the direction of the smoke trails and within seconds her five-foot four and a half frame was suddenly swallowed up in a sea of humanity that pressed in on her from all sides. Elizabeth began to flow with the crowd, carried off her feet as if by an ocean wave by the sweaty and anxious masses she was now deeply embedded within. Panicked, she couldn't take a breath to even yell for help. And then, like a tornado that picks up its victims in a violent tempest, only to set them down gently some distance away, she was back on the ground. The crowd having momentarily relaxed its grip on her.

Like a football running back, she saw her opening and drove herself through it. Eventually the crowd thinned enough that she could make out the upper floors of her hotel in the distance. She slowed to a brisk walk and her heart palpitations died down. What had she gotten herself into? But it's okay. She was going to make it. And that's a good thing because what would Carson and Jacob have thought of her lying to them about being in Taiwan instead of Beijing when they flew her body back home from Beijing?

Bangs and arc light flashes from Tiananmen Square ricocheted off the buildings lining Chang An Avenue. She prayed they were only fireworks. They weren't.

Elizabeth was at ground zero for the maelstrom that was about to hit Chang An Avenue. She turned around to look. The tens of thousands of people who'd been milling about Tiananmen Square and Chang An Avenue suddenly turned in unison away from the square and began running her way. Once again, she was suddenly overtaken by a rush of frantic humanity who arrived from the shooting in Tiananmen Square running for their lives—some at full tilt, some injured and limping. At once everyone around her realized what was happening and panic engulfed the entire street. Some were trampled. The staccato of gun fire became constant.

Elizabeth turned and made a beeline for her hotel— *don't look back*—but the crowd knocked her from her feet several times. On the final occasion she had to pick herself up from the street, pedicabs and carts carrying bloody bodies were bringing up the rear of the horrific parade. She knew first aid and reached out to help a Chinese teen who was piled atop a half dozen others on a donkey cart, all writhing, screaming and covered in blood. That was when Elizabeth heard a sound that she would never forget: the distinct thud of bullets impacting human flesh as they raked across several of the people standing nearby. And struck once again, the teen. He was dead.

Elizabeth turned one last time to look at what was coming in the distance: across the now open street a row of soldiers were emerging from the smoke—flashes coming from the end of their rifle barrels. Bullets whizzed all around. It was only a matter of seconds now: she was about to die. *God, if now is my time, take me. I am Yours.* She crossed herself. *So Lord, I'm just going to walk back to my hotel now.* And she did just that. She straightened her jacket, pulled her purse strap over her shoulder, turned her back on the soldiers and began calmly walking away in prayer: *Yea, though I walk through the valley of the shadow of death, I will fear no evil: for thou art with me; thy rod and thy staff they comfort me...*

Dazed, and having lost all track of time, she found herself at the main entrance to the Beijing Hotel, now behind a phalanx of Chinese soldiers with AK-47s who were standing guard. Elizabeth was counting on her age, western face and holding up her passport and room key gaining her entry. An officer came over and took her passport, looked at the picture, then at her. He nodded to his soldiers to let her through.

Once inside, she recited under her breath: "Stay in the hotel, Elizabeth." There was a message for her at the front desk—perhaps it was the Company checking in on her. Rather, Elizabeth's breakfast appointment had cancelled: *no kidding!* What the heck was *she* doing here?

Elizabeth retreated to her room, shaking from head to toe. Sitting on her bed in the dark, contemplating her near-death experience, her hotel room window continued to be lit by flashes and her nervous system shaken by loud bangs. She continued praying.

A volley of bullet impacts crawled across the side of the hotel until they shattered her balcony's sliding glass door. She fell back into her room and crawled to her bathroom, closing and locking the door behind her.

Shivering in near total darkness she felt wetness on her arm. Remaining crouched on the floor, she reached up and switched on the light. It was blood. Her arm had a one-inch cut that was bleeding. It wasn't a bullet hole, she knew that much. It must have been flying glass, she concluded. She pulled a face towel down to her and wrapped her arm, never leaving the relative security of the tile floor. She got the bleeding under control.

After things had quieted down outside her curiosity overwhelmed her. She emerged from the bathroom to find the curtains to the balcony gently waving in the breeze. There were bullet holes in her room's inner wall. She swallowed hard at how close she'd come to death that night. She told herself she shouldn't dare go back to the balcony to see what was happening. She didn't listen to herself.

The masses were gone. Bright lights atop tanks coming down Chang An Avenue toward the square lit soldiers who were pulling bodies to the side of the avenue for collection. She somehow needed to get to the airport. Just then, there was a knock at the door. It was one of the hotel's security officers with a soldier standing on either side.

"Are you injured?" The security officer asked when he saw Elizabeth's arm wrapped in the towel.

"I'm fine. I just want to get to the airport."

"We are arranging transportation now for all our guests. We will be back to collect you in 30 minutes. Hand carry luggage only. No suitcases. Understand? Thirty minutes."

"Are you injured?" she was asked again by an employee of the Lido Hotel, whose circular domed lobby and reception area resembled a refugee camp of people from all the world's nationalities. Evidently, located halfway between Tiananmen Square and the Beijing Airport, it was being used as a staging area for foreigner evacuation. "You are injured."

"Yes, just little. From flying glass I guess. But it is not serious. I just need a place to wash up. And some bandages would be nice."

The woman led Elizabeth to a corridor where all the hotel room doors were open. Easily a hundred people were milling about the hallway and between the rooms. Elizabeth was able to get to a sink where she could properly tend to her wounds. After washing off the dried blood, she could see that there was no serious penetration. She bandaged her wound.

When she returned to the lobby she saw the lobby restaurant's daily-special sign board was pressed into the service by U.S. Embassy personnel, who erased the words: "Western Buffet Breakfast: FEC 88 + 15% Service Charge," and wrote: "American Citizen Collection Point."

"Attention, U.S. Citizens," a U.S. Embassy staffer announced to the crowd. "We cannot confirm the reports that there may still be airplanes at the airport. But we've been informed that our government has leased four jumbo jets to come to Beijing to evacuate its citizens. We are now locating ground transportation and will be taking people to the airport according to number. We ask for your patience and cooperation."

Upon hearing the announcement a sense of joy welled up from deep within Elizabeth's chest from hearing an American accent. She flashed her passport to an embassy staffer, who then gave her a slip of paper with the U.S. Embassy seal and a hand-written number on it.

After making herself comfortable with the pillows and blankets that the hotel staff had made available in the lobby, she looked around to see the forlorn faces of the men and women sheltering there. Some had blood on their clothing, others arms in slings. But most were terrified expat families like hers, huddled together on the floor awaiting evacuation. Elizabeth locked eyes with a man who she instantly recognized as an agent she'd provided identity, travel and business documents to a year earlier—when she was based in Spain. When their eyes met, they acknowledged each other. Like her, he had blood on his clothes.

The room fell silent and all heads turned in unison to the main doors as a group of ten Chinese soldiers entered, led by three men in street clothes. The soldiers instantly deployed around the circular lobby, blocking all doorways. Each of the three men in street clothes held up a photo as they slowly walked around the room comparing faces to the photos. One stopped in front of a man, pointed his finger and ordered two guards to bring him to his feet. He was handcuffed. Everyone in the room was absolutely terrified, none more than Elizabeth. The second one seemed unable to find a match for his photo. But the third one stopped in front of the agent. He reached out his hand and said in English: "Passport." The agent shrugged. He had nothing with him but the clothes on his back. The man in plain clothes pointed his finger at the agent and ordered two guards to bring him to his feet.

Ensuring their backs were turned, Elizabeth grabbed the water bottle of the person sitting next to her, quickly leapt to her feet, and walked briskly across the room. "Honey? Honey? Wait, wait. What's going on?"

One of the plain clothed men put his hand up to stop her. "This is not your business."

"The heck it isn't. This is my husband." She said. "I was just getting him a drink of water."

"He is under arrest."

"For what? We're tourists."

"He is under arrest. Matches description and no passport or identification."

"But he is my husband. He lost all his things when we started running. We were there taking pictures one minute and the next hundreds of people pushed past us. I got hurt when I fell," she held out her bandaged arm. "But I managed to hang on to my passport. Here," Elizabeth took her passport out of her purse and handed it to him.

"We are James and Beth Osborn. We live in Singapore. We're just tourists. Here, look," She pulled out an envelope: a Singtel Telecom phone bill addressed to Mr. and Mrs. James Osborn.

The plain clothed man quickly pulled the envelope from her hand. He first looked at the envelope, then agent. "What street do you live on?" He asked the agent.

Dead silence in the room. Distant automatic gunfire could be heard through the window, amid police sirens.

Elizabeth's heart raced, the veins in her neck throbbing, she became slightly lightheaded. If the agent didn't know his own street address, it would prove them both liars. And they both would be immediately arrested. In a flash, she saw Carson standing by the Corpus Christi fountain. Jacob when he was first brought to her in the delivery room. Her father playing acoustic guitar, singing she and her siblings to sleep. She may have just done the most stupid thing of her entire life. She prayed with all her heart that the agent had not only been to the CIA's Singapore office, but actually remembered the street address.

The agent paused, looked at Elizabeth who was on the verge of fainting, then flashed her a glint of a grin. "Upper Thompson Road," the agent replied to the plain clothed man, as if he were peeved at being asked. "114 Upper Thompson Road."

* * *

"It was the craziest thing. The wind was howling and all of a sudden the glass window I was sitting nearby shattered," she said to Carson as he drove her home from Singapore's Changi Airport.

"It sounds like the glass wasn't properly tempered…if it were tempered at all," Carson responded. "Do they even temper glass in Taiwan? I don't know. At least you didn't get shards in your eye."

"Yes," Elizabeth said, looking out the window. "Very lucky."

"At least you weren't in Beijing!" Carson said, shaking his head.

"I'm not ready to work with China just yet…and now, after Tiananmen Square, maybe never."

Carson was the best listener in the world, but Elizabeth couldn't tell him a thing. And there was so much to tell him. The Company offered PTSD counseling, but Elizabeth attended only two sessions before she dropped it. Given everything she'd been through in her life, she could teach the therapist a thing or two. But Elizabeth couldn't hide the nightmares from Carson. She always managed to come up with a good excuse each time, though. For the months that they lasted.

* * *

A year later, in 1990, Elizabeth concluded that she'd never become accustomed to flying into Hong Kong's Kai Tak Airport at night: she would always and forever be enthralled by it. As her plane made its descent into Hong Kong, the city's oasis of lights contrasted starkly with the abject blackness unique to flying over the ocean on a moonless night. But instead of continuing to the outskirts of the city, where most airports are, they flew straight into the heart of the city, as though their plane were landing in New York's Central Park.

Their final approach to Kai Tak Airport required the plane to pitch sharply while rolling to the right in order to line up with the runway that jutted into Hong Kong's Harbor. Skimming the tops of buildings at that angle, Elizabeth was able to see into the windows of Kowloon's low-rise buildings off the starboard side, and she grinned at the sight of a bather toweling off through his apartment window.

Early the next morning Hong Kong Deputy Station Chief Ken Wilkenson picked her up from her hotel. Ken was a quirky guy, in his mid-thirties, balding, and always wore a three-piece suit. She also noticed that he would develop a funny twitch in his cheek when he became stressed or frustrated. They were headed to the CIA's Lowu House: A three-story mansion among a row of similar mansions along a ridge overlooking the Hong

Kong-China Lo Wu border KCR rail station.

When she first arrive there, she noted to Wilkenson that nearly all of the houses flew the Nationalist Flag of the Republic of China. "A die-hard Nationalist neighborhood, I see."

"Sometimes the best place to hide is in plain sight," was his explanation.

They pulled their ID badges from their pockets for scanning, then walked up stairs. It was apparent to anyone that the house was in fact a working office. It was loaded with several mainframe computers, numerous terminals, and a variety of electronic equipment, all manned by more than a dozen employees. When they reached the third floor, they walked down a hall and directly into a window-less conference room that had a large wall-to-wall mirror on one side.

"This is agent Curtiss Bradley," Wilkenson said, introducing the mid-20s American man who was waiting for them. "Mr. Bradly is the one headed to Fujian Province soon. Please, make him ready for travel."

After exchanging pleasantries they discussed his cover: he was to be a highly trained technician who repairs textile machines made in North Carolina. A customer in Fujian Province, a textile mill, had a machine that needed repair. Elizabeth did not have sufficient clearance to know what his actual mission was, but after what she'd experienced in Beijing she knew all missions in China were inherently dangerous. She then began running through her checklist. Passport with corresponding travel stamps: handed over. Matching business cards: done. Diagnostic tools and tool bag, plus two work shirts with his first name and his company name on it: check.

When they were finished Curtiss and Elizabeth discovered that they were both in Beijing the night of June 3rd. And, that both of them were on Chang An Avenue when the shooting began. Both had suffered injuries in the ordeal—Curtiss while on Chang An Avenue had sustained bullet fragments to his shins.

"It happened before I was an agent," he explained. "I was with a young lady, from a village I had stayed in. She was a university student. I was living with her family and she insisted on going to Beijing for the protests," his jaw muscles tightened as he paused to decide what to say next. "I went there with her to protect her. I promised her family that I would. She died in my arms."

As she did for every one of the agents she prepped, Elizabeth said a small silent prayer to God to protect them from danger.

After three consecutive days at the Lowu house preparing five sets of separate identities and travel documents, Elizabeth was ready to go home. But before returning to Singapore the next day, she was to be one of the guests of honor at an awards ceremony hosted by the visiting Director. It was five o'clock when she arrived at the Lowu House's third-floor to find the corridor outside the conference room occupied by the entire Hong Kong Station, all with plastic glasses of red or white wine in their hands. When the door to the conference room finally opened, the Director stood at the entrance and shook everyone's hand as they walked in one by one, introducing themselves. Wilkenson stood beside a podium that had been set up at the far end of the room.

"Is everyone here?" The Director asked Wilkenson when the last hand had been shaken.

Wilkenson nodded.

"Ladies and gentlemen, as you all know, in spite of having significant assets on the ground in the PRC, this station incurred zero casualties in last year's Tiananmen Square incident." The Director paused for applause. Elizabeth was the third of five agents and specialists who were receiving letters of commendation that day.

The Director removed his reading glasses, filed them in his suit breast pocket and searched the audience. "This next letter of commendation is for Elizabeth Jordon—mind you she's a specialist not trained for covert missions of this nature—who used instinctive quick thinking, selflessness and a whole lot of courage, to save one of our top agents from arrest."

Amid more applause, Elizabeth made her way to the podium when the Director called for her. She stood with the Director for a photo, then beside him. "It is my honor to present Elizabeth Jordon with this letter of commendation..." As the Director pulled his reading glasses from his suit breast pocket, donned them and began to read from the letter, Elizabeth heard her Aunt Estelle's voice in her mind: *So, now what do you have to say for yourself?*

* * *

Carson had a conference call with Ipswich headquarters scheduled for the evening Elizabeth returned from Hong Kong, and so wasn't able to pick her up from the airport. Elizabeth paid the taxi driver, slung her simply-too-heavy carry-on bag over her shoulder, pulled her rolling luggage along behind her and pushed the button of her apartment's underground carpark elevator. She'd had quite enough of travel for the moment, and the elevator ride seemed to take forever just to reach her floor.

Carson was well trained and kept the apartment neat for the four days she was away in Hong Kong, or at least cleaned up in time for her return—save a couple of dishes hiding in the kitchen sink. She'd get to them in the morning.

Elizabeth could hear Carson's conversation on speakerphone as she entered the hallway. The door to the home office was cracked open and she could see him in there, unaware that she had returned home. Continuing on down the hall to their bedroom Elizabeth made a mental note that she couldn't forget to leave her letter of commendation at the office the next day—lest Carson or Jacob accidentally find it one day. She had finished prepping for her weekly radio show on the flight from Hong Kong, so that was out of the way. She was ready to broadcast the next morning—technology now allowing her to do that from their home office.

At this level of exhaustion, a shower was out of the question. She quickly changed, brushed her teeth, went to bed and fell asleep.

CHAPTER 8

Jacob and his wife Janet had flown in from their home in Cincinnati Ohio to join Elizabeth and Carson for Christmas '92 at the family's favorite resort on Tioman Island. Janet was four months pregnant and jetlagged, and was taking a nap inside their seaside bungalow while Elizabeth, Carson and Jacob watched the sunset together on the porch over chilled white wine.

"Where was your favorite place growing up?" Elizabeth asked Jacob.

"I'd have to say Woodbridge. I loved living on Aunt Theresa's estate."

"Yeah, us too," Elizabeth and Carson said in unison. Elizabeth retold her sunglasses and the ghost story. "I miss having an English ghost around too."

"You two seem pretty well settled in Singapore now."

Carson and Elizabeth looked at each other and shrugged. "Well, it's a terrific city, and we have some great friends here. Your mother travels too much..."

"...we don't like the idea being so far away from you and Janet, and our future grandchild," Elizabeth finished.

"I don't know," Carson stretched. Sighing: "Maybe I ought to do something about that."

"Oh, please," Elizabeth chided. "You've been trying

to move us back stateside for the past ten years now."

Elizabeth took the occasion to reminded Jacob. "Speaking of stateside, don't forget: I'm visiting the end of February. I'll be attending a broadcaster's convention in New York City and will swing by Cincinnati on the way back."

Jacob nodded that he'd been duly reminded. "Madrid was pretty awesome too."

"I did play a heck of a lot of golf there," confessed Carson.

There was laughter, there were thoughtful pauses and there were moments of sheer joy as the Jordon family strolled through their life together as expats while the last sliver of sun slipped over the horizon and painted the western sky with streaks of warm yellow sunlight.

As the day bowed out gracefully to allow the first stars of night to make their debut, Elizabeth pondered the moment. As she listened to Carson and Jacob talking she thought that perhaps this was the time to tell them. Jacob was grown up and surely could be trusted to keep a secret. Carson, not so grown up, but at least he too has been known to keep a secret. She decided: This was the right moment to tell the boys the truth.

"I have something important to tell you."

Carson and Jacob stopped laughing about whatever they were finding amusing and looked seriously at Elizabeth.

"I've been wanting to tell you this…but I couldn't."

Carson and Jacob looked at each other, then at Elizabeth. Their smiles were gone.

"I've been lying to both of you, to everyone. And I simply can't stand it anymore. I have to let you know the truth."

Carson and Jacob now looked at her with dead seriousness.

"I've been working for the CIA for the past ten years. Lady Avebury recruited me—she is the *grand dame* of the spy business in Europe. My radio show? A front for sending coded message behind the Iron Curtain, and into Afghanistan and now countries like China and Vietnam. My relocation business is real, but for relocating agents with their covert identities around the world."

Elizabeth was met with silent stares.

"Every move we've made after England wasn't because *Carson* was being relocated. It was because *I* was being relocated. Lady Avebury was pulling all the strings at Leith Sports & Leisure to make it seem we were being relocated for Carson." Elizabeth thrust her arm forward. "This cut on my arm? Oh, it was from flying glass alright. But shattering glass from bullets fired in Tiananmen Square. I was nearly killed that night and only escaped Beijing by the skin of my teeth."

Carson and Jacob were transfixed on Elizabeth.

"Now this is important: I've been sworn to secrecy about what I do. And now that I've told you, you can't breathe a word of what I've told you to another soul. Not even family."

Carson and Jacob looked back at each other. Silence.

"Aw, jeese Elizabeth! I thought you were going to announce that you had cancer or something," Carson burst out laughing. "You had us going there for a moment."

"Right, Aunt Theresa is a spy master and my mom is Jane Bond."

Both of them had a hearty laugh, but for some reason it didn't bother Elizabeth.

"I'm going to look in on Janet," Jacob said through a laugh, as he went over to give his mother a big hug. "I love you mom. You're the best." Humming the James Bond theme song, he disappeared behind the screen door.

Carson composed himself, slid closer to her on the porch swing and put his arm around her. "Honey, you don't have to make up stories about your life. We've had an extraordinary life together. You have always been an exciting and vibrant woman to me. I love you just the way you are." He gave her a big beautiful kiss before announcing that he was going inside to take a shower before supper.

Now alone on the porch with only the stars and the surf to keep her company Elizabeth smiled a knowing smile. Perhaps it was better that they didn't believe her. It was kind of like, hiding in plain sight. Besides, at least they can never say she never told them.

PREVIEW

"You picked a good year to come to our convention here in New York City, Elizabeth," the National Radio Broadcasters' Association Vice President informed her. "We have over a thousand participants signed up for this year's show. That's a record."

"I'm absolutely tickled to be here." And Elizabeth was. After ten years doing radio from four countries she had developed her own style and a decent following too. The NRBA Vice President was visiting Singapore, heard one of her shows, and invited her to New York to talk about syndication in some US markets—those with large Asian demographics. Their lunch at the World Trade Center's Windows On The World restaurant was the first of what Elizabeth hoped would be successful syndication negotiations.

It was a cold day in New York, at least for her, below freezing, and after living in Singapore where the average annual temperature is around 32 degrees centigrade (89 Fahrenheit) year-round, Elizabeth was highly susceptible to its effects. But she was prepared, her clothing—

sweater, under coat, over coat, hat, gloves, scarf, needed a separate chair just for themselves. The light snow falling outside the window of the 107th floor of the North Tower however, was a delightful treat for her, having not experienced snow for many years. She couldn't wait to get outside and enjoy it: there was something special about when it snowed in New York City.

Suddenly, the entire room violently shoved to one side, then snapped back to the other direction, knocking over her water glass and other top-heavy objects on their table. The lights went out. Screams came from all around them. "What the heck was that," the NRBA Vice President said grabbing the table for stability. The building snapped the same way again, and then again, at a frequency, as if they were at the end of a giant reverberating pole. Before the vibrations had fully dissipated, he was on his Motorola MicroTAC cellular phone calling his assistant. "She'll call back to tell us what's going on," he told Elizabeth.

"Ladies and gentleman," the restaurant manager raised his hands to calm the diners and staff. "We are safe here. The electricity is out, the elevators are on a separate circuit so we should be able to get down in an orderly..." The maitre d' walked up to the manager and whispered in his ear. "Sorry, the elevators aren't working either. So there is nothing to do but to wait here for the power to come back on."

The building shimmied. Elizabeth had been in plenty of high rise buildings in her time, even during typhoons in Singapore, but she never felt a building shimmy like the north tower was doing.

"But what happened? This isn't just a power outage. Something happened to the building," one patron questioned.

"We don't know, we're calling building manage..." another member of the staff approached the manager and only shrugged in the negative. "Okay, the phones are out too. Does anyone have a cellular phone that we can use to call down to building management?"

Elizabeth grabbed the NRBA Vice President's phone from his hand and rushed it over to the manager.

No answer.

He tried again.

No answer.

He tried again. "Its ringing but..." Elizabeth was close enough to hear the pandemonium on the other end of the phone after someone picked up. "This is Windows On The World, what's going on down there..." He turned and started walking to keep the conversation private. Elizabeth, and the others anxiously waiting there, stayed put and let him do his job.

The building shimmied again.

He returned pale and with a blank look on his face. "I understand. Please keep us advised through this number." He flipped the phone closed. "Ladies and gentlemen. There has been an explosion in the underground parking garage of the building." Two women screamed. "I've been assured that we are in no danger. The structural strength of this building comes from the steel facing along the outside of the building. Therefore, we have very widespread load bearing structures that a single explosion would be near impossible to knock out.

"What was it? A bomb?" a borderline hysterical woman asked as the building shimmied once again.

"We only know it was an explosion. Underground. In the parking garage beneath the..."

Screams erupted again when pitch black smoke began seeping through the elevator doors and air vents at the top of the room.

Elizabeth's gut immediately warned her that she and those people in that restaurant were in big trouble.

ABOUT THE AUTHOR

Kathryn Raaker, internationally syndicated radio and TV personality, has now lent her creative talents to launching this first book of her *Elizabeth Bromwell* series: *Chronicles of an Expat Spy*.

This fictional series is told in the sumptuous and exotic places of her own expatriate experience. Starting with her first international move to England in 1978, Kathryn lived in England, Spain, Turkey and Singapore over two decades. Her series' vibrant, unforgettable and bigger-than-life characters are composites from hundreds of fascinating people she met along the way.

Kathryn's co-author Lawrence Allen, author and recipient of *Let's Just Talk Radio's* 2014 Best Political Thriller of the Year award, lived as an expat for 20 years in Asia. Together, Kathryn and Lawrence bring Elizabeth Bromwell to life.

Made in the USA
Columbia, SC
11 March 2019